ARKA

THE PHILOSOPHY
OF MAGIC

Arthur Versluis has a long-standing interest in magic
as it relates to traditional culture. He has translated
the poetry and prose of Novalis and, while completing graduate studies in literature, has been writing
other works concerned with the Hermetic tradition,
including a novel based upon the life of Giordano
Bruno. A recipient of the Hopwood Award in
Literature, he currently lives in Ann Arbor,
Michigan.

THE PHILOSOPHY
OF MAGIC

ARTHUR VERSLUIS

ARKANA

BOSTON, LONDON AND HENLEY

First published in 1986
by ARKANA PAPERBACKS
ARKANA PAPERBACKS is an imprint of
Routledge & Kegan Paul plc

9 Park Street, Boston, Mass. 02108, USA

14 Leicester Square, London WC2H 7PH, England and

Broadway House, Newtown Road,
Henley on Thames, Oxon RG9 1EN, England

Set in 10/11 point Sabon
by Columns of Reading
and printed in Great Britain by
Clays Ltd, St Ives plc

2

Library of Congress Cataloging in Publication Data

Versluis, Arthur, 1959-

The philosophy of magic.
Bibliography: p.
Includes index.
1. Hermetism. I. Title.
BF1611.V47   1986   299'.93   85-15673

British Library CIP Data also available

Magic is the book of all scholars. All that will learn must first learn Magic, be it a high or lowly art. Even the peasant in the field must go to the magical school, if he would cultivate his field.

Magic is the best theology, for in it true faith is both grounded and found. And he is a fool that reviles it, for he knows it not, and blasphemes against both God and himself, and is more a juggler than a theologian of understanding.

Jacob Böehme

CONTENTS

ILLUSTRATIONS

ILLUSTRATIONS

PREFACE

Before beginning this study proper, it is necessary to clarify several matters, not the least of which is the relation of magic and alchemy to our present era, and to the traditional cultures. This work, needless to say, draws from and is meant to refer exclusively to these subjects as they are found in the traditional cultures, of which they are a natural part. However, because our present society is anything but traditional, and because the traditional framework or 'mesocosms' within which magic and alchemy arose and were transmitted no longer exist, they appear to us as isolated, out of context as it were, and so we observe them from the inferior point of view – as phenomena – rather than as aspects of the primordial culture.

This work, then, is an attempt to show how these exist within the structure of the primordial culture by setting forth some of the traditional cosmology upon which magic and alchemy are based, and relating them to it. It is, in other words, in a very real sense a *retrospective*, since the progressive destruction of the traditional cultures necessarily implies the progressive disappearance of these aspects of tradition as well. In fact, this point cannot be emphasized enough: that strange as it might seem at first glance, magic and alchemy cannot exist per se outside the traditional culture and without the 'protective shell' of orthodox religion, with which they are necessarily bound. For this reason, to the extent that magic and alchemy exist outside a tradition are they – as is the traditional orthodoxy – increasingly subject to malevolent and infernal influences, manifested in greed in the former case and hatred in the latter.[1]

And so we can see why it is that any egregious individual forays into these areas in our present time are very likely to involve one with forces that can only be termed infernal, as the 'protecting shell' of the traditional no longer in general obtains for such disciplines, extending by and large only to those within certain bounds because of the weakening influences of and behind modern society. It must also be emphasized that although in this study we approach magic and alchemy in their highest manifestations as byproducts or aspects of spiritual discipline in the traditional cultures, the production of unusual phenomena can by no means be taken to represent spiritual 'progress,' for such effects belong to the sensory realm, the nature of which is traditionally seen to be that of maya, of deception. And given the impetus of our present era toward blindness to all but the merely phenomenal world, given the inherently deceptive nature of that realm, and given the prophecies found in the Surangama Sutra as in the New Testament of those who would, if it were possible, deceive even the elect with wonders, it would indisputably be wisest to adhere as closely as possible to those orthodox religious traditions which alone can continue the stream of the primordial Tradition.

Although we have here adduced instances from traditional literature to illustrate the traditional cosmology which underlies such phenomena, these instances are just that – for in all Eastern teachings it is said that phenomena may occur on the Path, but to cling to it, to attach value to it in itself, is a great hindrance. One must always bear in mind that the Transcendent is by definition beyond phenomenal characteristics, whereas the 'essence', so to speak, of Error is deformity and illusion.

There is at present a superficial modern reaction against the gross materialism which has prevailed in the West for some time, a reaction which, conditioned by the prevalent Cartesian dualism, takes the form of embracing all non-material realms as amorphously spiritual and beneficent. This tendency is marked by an *attachment* to 'phenomena,' and can well result –

because the modern era has consisted in a 'hardening' against the Divine protection which traditional cultures afforded those within their sphere – in the 'unchaining' of the inferior or infernal forces against which modern man has virtually no higher protection, having cut himself off from the traditional.

Given present tendencies and conditions, then, it is not hard to extrapolate a future conjunction between manipulative science and the proliferating false or counter-traditions – prefigured by 'parapsychology' and the advent of computers and artificial intelligence on one hand, and false or mock-mysticism on the other[2] – which can only lead to absolute solipsism (insofar as such an ultimate illusion is possible) and to the final dissolution or atomization which will conclude the present maha-yuga, or Great Year.

With all this in mind – and remembering also that at the ending of an age even those with the best of intentions are adversely affected – we can only but continue on the Way as best we can, using authentic Tradition as our guide.

And so we begin our study, keeping in mind at all times, however, that we refer to magic and alchemy not in terms of the darkness of the present era, but only within the context of the traditional cultures and as byproducts of the spiritual path and Primordial Tradition which is at the essence of those cultures.[3] For without that Tradition, these are as wholly lost to us as we ourselves.

ACKNOWLEDGMENTS

Among the people invaluable in the preparation of this work were Dennis Keller – for his suggestions, his observations, and his friendship – and Barbara Versluis, for the illustrations and for her patience, without either of whom it would not have taken its present form.

Grateful acknowledgment must be made, too, to the University of Michigan Press for their permission to quote from their edition of Jacob Böehme's *Six Theosophical Points*, as to the Akademische Druck-u. Verlagsanstalt for their gracious permission to reproduce illustrations from their fine edition of *de Occulta Philosophia* by Henry Cornelius Agrippa, edited by Karl Nowotny (Graz, 1967), though most of the illustrations, with the exception of the table of correspondences and the calendars of Trithemius, were adapted by B. Versluis.

Permission was also granted by Yale University Press to reproduce the sigil and mantra on page 72, taken from *The Teachings of Taoist Master Chuang* by Michael Saso (New Haven, 1976). The Tibetan Buddhist iconographic drawings and correspondences were modeled after those of Pierre Rambach in *The Secret Message of Tantric Buddhism* (New York, 1979).

INTRODUCTION

Magic and alchemy have borne a great deal of calumny over the centuries, and at present they lie largely discarded and ignored as the effluvia of the past, relics of times and cultures long since superseded by logic in the triumphant march of modern man toward an obviously radiant future, albeit one marked so to speak by fear, disintegration and destruction. And no doubt, given the circumstances of the modern era, it would be best if magic and alchemy were to continue to be regarded as mere superstition, rather than as practices in themselves which might be followed outside the protective mantle of tradition. But because of the dissolving effect which constitutes the modern era − because the remnants of magical and alchemical texts and teachings still exist, but are 'divorced' by modern observers from their wider traditional context − a situation has arisen in which magic and alchemy are regarded as disciplines in themselves, rather than being manifestations one encounters when traveling along a traditional religious Path.

As a result, one can see today a situation arising which involves the greatest possible danger to those who misguidedly become involved with 'pseudo-traditional mysticism' or 'neo-shamanism', not recognizing that these are, for reasons we will discuss later, but 'inverted' images of the traditional, be it

Buddhist, Islamic or Christian, and can well lead to the psyche becoming irremediably lost in the labyrinthine confusion of the 'second world.'[1]

Because of these circumstances, it becomes necessary to examine the philosophy and cosmology upon which the magical and alchemical vision of the cosmos was based, in order that this vision might be seen whole, as it arose and was transmitted within traditional cultures, rather than as at present 'decapitated' and feeding the illusion of ego, the delusions of psyche. For although there are a welter of books available on the history and external ritual, the lore and superficial aspects of magic and alchemy, whether sympathetic or hostile, mocking or serious, virtually all leave one dissatisfied; in reading them one knows that there was, clearly, something most essential behind the quests of the alchemists and the rituals of the magi. But what?

It seems that what we need, more than another compendium or history, is an examination of the alchemical and Hermetic vision seen in its entirety, so that magic and alchemy are seen for what they are: not as ends in themselves, nor as means to any end, but rather as the natural effects and symbolism of traditional spiritual discipline. It is that which this study – by no means exhaustive – seeks to do. For the pursuit of magic and alchemy in themselves, as either means or end, needless to say belongs to the realm of the ego, of desire; hence it is ironic indeed that it is only when such pursuit is abandoned in favor of the traditional spiritual path that the true magic, the true alchemy is revealed in the transmutation of the self.[2]

It is the relation of that which we call magic and alchemy to this spiritual transmutation which alone can provide a unified understanding of them, both being but manifestations of the path toward the 'one thing needful.' That this is so is suggested even by the simple fact that magic and alchemy are found worldwide, in all traditional cultures – in remarkably similar manifestations – a uniformity which can ultimately only result from the single unifying aim of those cultures: spiritual realization.

Although it is difficult for us – bound as we are by the dualistic, Cartesian view of existence as consisting in the purely physical and in external series of coincidence – to rightly understand the more organic and unified vision of the traditional cultures, reflected in the West by the Hermetic tradition, it is precisely this which is most necessary, for it is only within such a tradition that magic and alchemy arose, and through which they can be understood.

A common modern assumption has been that magic and alchemy were at best merely haphazard collections of superstition compiled by people ignorant of the rational, physical laws, when in fact magic and alchemy are based upon suprarational laws and principles of which modern man is in general unaware. In short, the abyss between modern beliefs and the vision of traditional cultures arose not because of the supposed ignorance of the latter – which were in truth not nearly so concerned with the workings of the physical world as in theirs, and our, celestial Origin – but rather this abyss results in large part from the general eclipse of the Pythagorean, Hermetic and Neoplatonic understanding of the cosmos, in which Western magic arose and was transmitted.

In fact, a distinct historical pattern of division (di-vision) can be traced in the West, a splitting into two camps as it were; on the one hand, one has the orthodox religious form which tended to ignore the necessity of individual spiritual transmutation, and on the other, the solitary magus or alchemist, who often tended to ignore the necessity of traditional religious form. As a result, both diverged into materialistic or egoistic paths: the Church extended itself into political and economic spheres, while the magus or alchemist often erroneously sought personal power and riches by regarding magic or alchemy as means, not merely effects contingent upon and enclosed within, the higher aim of the primordial tradition. This divergence eventually resulted in the grossest of distortions: orthodoxy came to be identified with those who murdered hundreds of thousands accused of magic at the one extreme (the confusion of spiritual authority with temporal power), while alchemy and magic came to be seen as the attempts of the greedy to literally transmute lead into gold, or to gain riches and power, or to wield evil influence. Both tendencies result from the same misguided literalization, and consequent polarization, of that which was unified and harmonious within the traditional culture. But simply because the two extremes eventually came to resemble their caricatures of one another does not mean that they were not, originally and within all traditional cultures, aspects of the same essential spiritual transmutation, magic being one discipline among many subsumed to that transmutation, alchemy being its symbology, and orthodoxy being its formal representation.

For in fact, a study of anyone who began to move toward a more profound understanding of the cosmos would reveal one who either tacitly or openly embraced the magical vision of existence. From the Pythagoreans to the Taoists, from Tibetan Buddhism to Hindu Tantrism, from the Platonists to the Sūfis, magic and alchemy are intimately related to the heart of the teaching, being but external manifestations of inner spiritual transformation – byproducts as it were. Even an Aristotelian like Avicenna[3] has been shown to have couched his Sūfi thought in Peripatetic terms. And it is only now being rediscovered that the essence of the Renaissance was to be found in the works of Marsilio Ficino and Pico della Mirandola, Henry Cornelius Agrippa, Giordano Bruno, Raymond Lull, Dr John Dee and Sir Edward Kelly.[4] These, the Hermetic 'magicians', were the ones who searched out and made more widely known the writings of the Greeks – Neoplatonic and Pythagorean – in their quest for, and revelation of, the traditional teachings insofar as they still existed in the West. Their aim, as manifested in Pico and Bruno's appeals to the Pope in particular, was to reunite orthodoxy and the magical vision under the original Hermetic tradition.

However, this was not to be. And hence the modern, flat view of the world as an external mass of matter evolved from chaos, with all its destructive consequences, arose when the magical vision of Bruno and Dee, of Lull and Fludd was suppressed in favor of the logical, categorical Aristotelianism of succeeding generations.

After the Renaissance magicians and Hermetic philosophers came the Romantic poets who, while for the most part not direct proponents of the Hermetic vision in the way that Pico and Bruno were, were nonetheless immersed in many of its aspects and carried on much of its understanding, its cosmology. In Wordsworth we see echoes of an animated Nature, the rolling rhythms of the land fading away before the jaded, two-dimensional industrial age: in Wordsworth and in Coleridge we see nostalgia for a world in which they could no longer take part. Wordsworth's 'pantheism,' Coleridge's omens and dreamlike visions, as of Kubla Khan, Blake's and Shelley's titans and mythological creations, Nerval's tarot symbolism and his trip to Egypt, Novalis's alchemical and Hermetic symbolism,[5] Yeat's 'gyres' – the list is long indeed. Rimbaud, Baudelaire, Victor Hugo all sought, as Rimbaud so explicitly said, to restore alchemy in the word, to create a new magic through poetry, since the old magic was so apparently gone. The attraction of all of these poets was not only in their literary ability but also, and perhaps more, in their successive attempts to reintroduce the Hermetic vision of the world, of which magic and alchemy are inevitably a part.

The Romantic poets, then, stand as it were midway between two worlds: behind them is the unified traditional realm, represented by the Hermetic teachings, while ahead of them is the modern era, the underlying 'aim' of which can also be personified in the form of the magus – albeit in this case, rather than uniting the realms, each seeks to be sole creator, sole manipulator, to usurp the place of the Divine rather than to fulfill it, and so in the end must meet with inevitable dissolution. In this lies much of the fascination which the Romantics hold for us: in them we can see the traditional past in which man *fulfills* the Divine, and in them we can see the future in which he seeks to *be* divine, the latter being an inversion of the former which might well be termed 'satanic'. In this distinction, too, we can see the difference between the forms of magic called 'white' and 'black': in the former we can see the traditional past; in the latter we can see the culmination of the modern era in a kind of historical continuum.

Hence, in order to understand the nature and place of magic within the traditional culture, we must first of all relinquish many of the modern preconceptions about it, not least of which is the artificial separation of 'orthodox religion' on the one hand, and 'magic and alchemy' on the other, for inasmuch as each is seen as separate from traditional spiritual discipline can they be rightly characterized as evil – that is, as furthering egotism. Without an understanding of the former, one cannot truly understand the latter, and vice versa – and it is for this reason that we devote time to the traditional understanding of magic and alchemy, and to the dispersion of misconceptions.

One such misconception is that magic implies belief. Of

course, in a sense it must, since without faith in the efficacy of something one would not undertake it, but at the same time it is absurd to think that the remarkable similarities among all traditional cultures arose by chance, and that magic and alchemy continued within them on the basis of mere belief, which as Plato observed in the *Republic* is but the inferior of knowledge, being based upon mere guessing, estimation and opinion. It is clear, then, that behind magic and alchemy there must be universal laws or principles at work – if there were not then nothing could be grouped under those headings to begin with! Magic, then, in its original form within a tradition must necessarily be a form of knowledge, of occurrences which take place according to given causes or conjunctions.

But at the same time it can be seen as the phenomena which occur occasionally to one who is on a traditional spiritual path, as a kind of byproduct, and so as a result we can say that just as all of the traditional disciplines can act as a reflection of and mode of transmission for spiritual transmutation – much like weaving, say, or the tea ceremony – so too can magic, with the proviso that magic also occupies an intermediate place, being a kind of arrested form of spiritual development, one concerned more with effects than with transformation of the self. This intermediate place accounts for much of the confusion which surrounds magic – but it is, and must be seen as, one traditional discipline among many.

A traditional discipline is one, generally speaking, into which one is born; it is a function within society which one fulfills, simultaneously fulfilling one's Divine nature: daily work, spiritual discipline form one harmonious whole. It is this – the traditional culture, which revolves as planets around a Sun – that Plato was describing in his *Republic*, though by that time such a culture had nearly vanished already in Greece, and has now virtually vanished from the world.

Thus, as for instance in Eskimo tradition, one does not so much choose to be a magician, but rather one simply finds that he *is* an anutquq: it is as it were his function.

With the traditional nature of magic as a discipline, a function in mind, we can see why it was that Plotinus – whose views seemed so similar to theirs superficially – felt compelled to condemn the Gnostic Christians in his famous treatise.[6] The Gnostics, he said, did not see man as part of the majestic tapestry of existence, but rather exalted him above all things. For them, magic consisted in compelling and manipulating nature and the celestial beings, when in truth magic operated only through divine sympathy and harmony – the traditional Hermetic teaching. Hence, according to Plotinus, the Gnostics sought to exalt themselves over all things – whereas in the traditional vision, of which magic is a part, all things become exalted through magic.

In this dispute we can see the true place of magic within the traditional culture – not as an egotistic means to power, but rather as the mediatrix, the harmonizing force within the culture, acting through *sympathy* in every sense of the word. The magus, within the tradition, acts as a harmonizer of the seen and the unseen, standing as he does between the purely 'religious' realm of the sage or saint and the culture and world as a whole. Perhaps more than any other discipline, then, magic is a *function* within the culture, acting to help resolve disputes, harmonize the weather, and in every way stabilize the realms.

And in this light we can see the resolution of the division into 'orthodoxy' and 'magic,' for just as within the individual sphere 'magical' phenomena or 'miracles' take place as the natural result of spiritual ascent or transmutation, acting for the greater good, so too in a pure culture the sage arises out of orthodoxy, who acts to preserve his teaching, while the magi as it were broadcast the benevolence of the Divine harmony which he revealed. Here too, then, we can see the meaning of the apocryphal tales in which the very search for base ends – as in the neophyte's search for the sword which will kill all his enemies, or Milarepa's practice of black magic – acts to transform the seeker, so that he who searches for the magic sword finds that ultimately he has been transformed into a saint, and cannot use the sword for ill even if he does obtain it.[7]

So we can see that spiritual transmutation, realization of Mind, lies at the heart of magic, as it lies at the heart of orthodoxy: magic is not so much a means to an end as it is a means to a higher means. Magic is in existence in every culture in the world – and is, in addition, strikingly unified despite the diversity of cultures – because it is a reflection of eternal principles and as such must exist so long as there are cultures. Contrary to the contentions of psychologists like Jung, Eastern wisdom and magic cannot be 'taken out of metaphysics and placed in psychological experience,'[8] for the essence of all traditional religion and magic lies precisely in the apprehension of that which is beyond and above the merely physical or psychological. To drag traditional metaphysics into the realm of the ego and the physical is to rob it of all power and value, forcing it in effect to affirm that which it must deny: the ultimate existence of the illusory ego.

Within the traditional culture, then, magic acts to demonstrate as well the illusory nature of the phenomenal world: it is we who are responsible for the dream we are living. As Chuang Tsu wrote: 'I dreamt I was a butterfly. When I awoke, I was not sure whether I was a man who had dreamed I was a butterfly, or a butterfly now dreaming I was a man.'[9] And in the Islamic tradition there is the story of the meeting between the philosopher Ibn Sīnā and the great Sūfi sage Abū Sa'īd. It is said that Abū Sa'īd asked Ibn Sīnā (Avicenna) whether a heavy body seeks the earth. 'Yes,' said Ibn Sīnā. Abū Sa'īd took a heavy vase and threw it in the air, where it stayed, unmoving. 'Why does it not fall?' asked Abū Sa'īd. 'A violent force is preventing it,' Ibn Sīnā answered. 'What is this violent force?' asked Abū Sa'īd. 'Your soul!' said Ibn Sīnā. 'Then purify your soul, so that you can do the same,' said Abū Sa'īd.[10] The story holds an esoteric meaning, in that in traditional symbology the vase characterizes the human body which is attached to the things of the earth, but it also illustrates why such phenomena appear within the traditional culture: in order to tantalize one – to draw all things – toward the Divine, in which all arises, all subsides, and all is a reflection.

In the Gnostic treatise entitled *Discourse on the Eighth and Ninth*, the Father Hermes Trismegistus guides his Son from the seventh sphere, the last of the temporal realms represented by the seven planets, which also mark the esoteric stages in alchemical – that is, spiritual – transmutation, into the eighth and ninth spheres of celestial Reality. As they ascend, they approach that which is beyond description, and he cries out:

> How shall I describe the universe? I am Mind and I see
> Mind, that which moves the soul! I see the one that moves
> me from pure forgetfulness. You give me power! I see myself!
> I want to speak! Fear restrains me. I have found the
> beginning of the power that is above all powers, the one that

has no beginning. I see a fountain bubbling with life. I have said, O my Son, that I am Mind. I have seen! Language is not able to reveal this. For the entire eighth, O my son, and the souls that are in it, and the angels, sing a hymn in silence. And I, Mind, understand.[11]

It is with this realization that all must begin – and end – the study of magic.

PART I

THE PHILOSOPHY
OF MAGIC

MIND

Although the collection of Hermetic documents now known as the *Poimandres* – documents pivotal in that enigmatic time termed the Renaissance[1] – are by no means the only, or even the major, explication of the traditional teaching of the three worlds of the cosmos, because they were the inspiration, the seed for so many western magicians, from Ficino to Fludd, we would do well to examine them in order to best delineate that philosophical understanding which informs every traditional cosmology, though of course with cultural variations. For while the *Corpus Hermeticum* was proven by M. Casaubon not to have been Egyptian in origin, both the Nag Hammadi finds and the content of the *Corpus* itself prove the authenticity and the antiquity of the teaching it puts forth, because in succinct form it reiterates the heart of traditional, magical understanding.

As we have seen, central to this understanding is the exclamation of the disciple in the *Discourse on the Eighth and Ninth*: 'I have seen! I am Mind!' In the *Corpus Hermeticum*, this realization is expanded upon in an even greater vision, so that the entire Hermetic cosmology is seen. The *Corpus* begins with the narrator, who is in a state of deep awareness, seeing an immense figure who asks his purpose. The narrator asked

10

who the other was, and he replied, 'I am Poimandres, the Mind (Nous) of absolute sovereignty.' The narrator then asked to be taught the nature of Being – Poimandres changed, and the boundless sky of light appeared.[2] This clear and limitless sky parallels that seen in Tibetan Buddhist teachings on the Clear Light, and that found in Jacob Böehme's *The Aurora*, all of which implies the awakening of the soul to its celestial Origin which appears to it as pure Light. The narrator of the *Corpus* then saw an obscurity spiraling downward which became wet, or humid Nature, uttered a groan, and after the Light uttered a cry, the Word came down to Nature while from Nature leapt the fire toward the Light, leaving earth, vapor and fire suspended by fire from the Light, shaking under the Breath. In this vision, then, we see both the creation of the macrocosm, and the awakening of the microcosm, or disciple, who through the purifying Fire rises back toward the light realizing the purpose of Creation.

'Fix your spirit on the Light,' said Poimandres, and when the narrator did so, he perceived the immense, the limitless Form (eidos) which preceded existence. Next he saw the second realm, the realm of breath and fire (Mercury and Sulphur), the elements and the seven planets, all in perfect harmony, creating an orderly and beautiful cosmos for the souls. The lowest, irrational sphere was inhabited by the birds, fish, reptiles and animals, as well as minerals and plants.

According to *Poimandres*, man was created in the image of the highest, the Divine sphere, passed through the celestial sphere of the planets and constellations, where he gained the proper aspect from each of the planets, until he reached the lowest of the planets – the moon. There he entered the realm of generation and, looking down into the water, he saw his own reflection, fell in love with it, and was drawn down into the irrational third sphere of matter and generation, now half animal, and half Divine.[3] Then it was that the bonds between things were severed, and creatures fell into the division of male and female, generation upon generation. And those people who knew the body to be transient, to come from darkness, rise up through the spheres upon death, in each sphere losing a particular irrational aspect, or vice, until they enter the eighth sphere – beyond the realm of the planets – where they bear the silent hymns of the Powers in the Father, (*Nous*) and finally themselves become Powers within Mind.

Poimandres then himself becomes a Power again, and the narrator is left to tell men of the truth he has witnessed.

In this first section of the *Corpus Hermeticum*, then, we have a remarkably condensed vision of the traditional three-world cosmology which is to be found in Neoplatonic teachings, in Gnostic Christian writings, in Qabalistic Judaism, in Islamic Sūfism, in Taoism and in esoteric Buddhism, varying with each tradition. There is the realm of the Ideal, the celestials, the realm of the planets, and the realm of samsara, of birth and death. The soul descends through these and then, when it is properly matured, disciplined, and enlightened, it 'ascends' toward Mind again, that which is beyond conception. Although the number of those who so 'ascend' is few, it is in truth for them that all creation exists in that they are its Pole, conducting the radiating pure Mind upon earth. In a sense, the *Poimandres* is an extremely condensed schematic in which the essential teaching of the traditional cosmology is unveiled, almost as if in compensation for the lack of direct transmission in the West.

The traditional cosmology can also be apprehended from the diagrams on pages 15–17 taken from the works of Robert Fludd, the seventeenth-century Hermetic physician and writer. In them we see the two major cosmological doctrines essential to an understanding of magic and alchemy: we see the depiction of man as microcosm, in whom is latent all the stages of existence, from pure Mind to the nox materia, and we see the emanation of all creation from the Light, through the cherubim and seraphim, the mediate realm of the planets and the elements, into the realm of earth, both doctrines we will examine later. But at the heart of magic and alchemy, Eastern and Western, is the teaching that all is Mind.

In the Lankavatara Sutra it is said: 'Mind is of Mind-only; no-Mind is also born of Mind; when understood, varieties of forms and appearances are of Mind only.' This same realization, as we have seen, was revealed in the *Corpus Hermeticum*, and can be approached, in terms of magic, as follows. Although we think that the phenomenal world of matter is permanent, is all that exists, it is not. Rather, each instant both it and we ourselves are different. The physical world is transient, constantly changing. It appears to remain stable only because it is informed by the Eternal, the higher Forms which are projected upon it. But this is not perceptible to the corporeal ego, which erroneously believes in the illusory duality between itself and the physical world, and which, in order to maintain that illusory duality, expends a great deal of habit energy in the constant recreation of that apparently constant world and ego.

Magic is none other than the dropping of this illusion, and of this habit energy, for to drop it implies freeing that energy – which normally is used to maintain our habitual world – in order to channel it toward the realization of the celestial realm. In other words, the perception of our daily world as external to us *is itself magic*, and illusory. We are in a sense already magicians, engaged in the continual recreation of our habitual worlds.

For even though matter is constantly changing, decaying and being reborn, the ego treats it as permanent in order to preserve the illusion that the ego itself has an independent existence. It constantly resorts to the accumulation of wealth, power and reputation in order to reiterate its own existence, and this accumulation and reiteration creates the habit energy. But since all this activity is confined to the lowest, physical sphere, it is but a striving after wind.

Magic is the recognition of this constant habitual recreation, and the consequent realization that the magician can in fact change his orientation from horizontal to vertical, in effect manifesting the celestial realm upon earth. That is to say, the magician manifests more pure aspects of being than those normally maintained through habit energy. As Jacob Böehme said, the celestial realm, being closer to the Divine Reality, and therefore freed from the bonds of space and time, appears as instantly changing images at play, and by reflecting that realm, the magician can in effect transcend the laws of space and time, since he is, through magic, realizing that which is beyond them.

How can this be? As Zen Master Dōgen said, being is none other than time.[4] Hence being exists only for a continuous series of instants, since, finally, time can be said to exist only in the moment of its perception, in the instant of realization of being. Being and time have their existence in Mind. The magician, by dropping the illusion of self and other, of ego and world, to that extent manifests the Mind in which being and time exist, and so is able to perform magic acts, acts which

13

transcend being and time. This should not be taken to mean, however, that the magician has achieved liberation from the realm of cause and effect. For the magician acts as a kind of filter, so that while he is manifesting Mind in a manner of speaking, he still maintains something of the illusion of self, which acts as a prism, creating different kinds of illusion than those normally seen through habit energy.

The magician still belongs to the realm of images, of appearances and manifestations, of *karma*, cause and effect, and in terms of the three-world cosmology, he is limited to a harmonizing of the psychic, second realm, and to the 'radiation' into the culture of the beneficient influences of the Ideal, celestial realm. For this reason, in Zen Buddhism all such manifestations are seen as *makyo*, or illusions, for they indicate that there is still something of self remaining. And as we have seen, in traditional cosmology, the purpose of existence is to manifest wholly upon earth the Sun of Mind, with no taint of ego blotting its radiance. Nonetheless, for magic and the magical vision of the world to be transcended there must first be something there to transcend.

As it is written in the Lankavatara Sutra, when one passes beyond habit energy, beyond the illusion of ego, beyond even images: 'All things are unborn and have nothing to do with being and nonbeing: all is nothing but Mind and is delivered from discrimination.'

Throughout the study of magic, one must keep this object – realization of Mind – wholly in sight.

If it is not, such study is worse than useless. For the realization of Mind is none other than ultimate compassion. And that is the seed, the emerald stone at the very heart of magic, its greatest secret and source of strength. Magic is, in its deepest sense, compassion. For in its true form, as mediatrix between the saint and the culture, it acts to radiate Mind.

This mediate realm or function, exclusive to magic as a discipline within the 'mandala' of a culture, is – just as is 'orthodox religion' – manifested through formal transmission: that is to say, through ritual. And hence it is to ritual – a central point at which 'orthodoxy' and 'magic' merge in the primordial tradition – that we now turn.

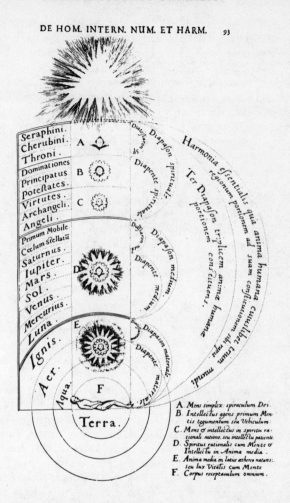

DE HOM. INTERN. NUM. ET HARM.   93

Seraphini.
Cherubini.
Throni.
Dominationes
Principatus
Potestates.
Virtutes.
Archangeli.
Angeli.
Primum Mobile
Cœlum Stellatū
Saturnus.
Iupiter.
Mars.
Sol.
Venus.
Mercurius.
Luna.
Ignis.
Aer.
Aqua.
Terra.

Harmonia essentialis qua anima humana cunctiliplex regionum portionem ad suam constituendam illi rupa
Ter Diapason triplicem animæ humanæ portionem conficiens.

Diapason spiritualis
Diapente spiritualis
Diapason medium
Diapente medium
Diapason materialis
Diapente materialis

A. *Mens simplex spiraculum Dei.*
B. *Intellectus agens primum Mentis tegumentum seu Vehiculum:*
C. *Mens & intellectus in spiritu rationali ratione, seu intellectu patiente.*
D. *Spiritus rationalis cum Mente & Intellectu in Anima media.*
E. *Anima media in latice æthereo natans: seu lux Vitalis cum Mente.*
F. *Corpus receptaculum omnium.*

I   Three illustrations conceived by and created for Robert Fludd, the English hermetic philosopher. The first depicts the three worlds and their relationships to the microcosm, the second does the same, representing their triadic unity, and the third – the *Causarum Universalum Speculum* – which can be read both clockwise and inwardly, shows the emanation of the cosmos. Note the numbers around the circumference, symbolizing the Pythagorean geometric harmony of the spheres

DE MUSIC. ANIM. COMPOS. PRAX. 275

cum nobilissimum, post corporis interitum & vinculorum vitæ à corpore, loco
nempe vilissimo, dissolutionem. Hujus autem harmoniæ humanæ descriptio-
nem, comparando illam cum mundana, hoc modo secundum cujuslibet illius
regionis differentiam, mundo accommodatam, delineavimus.

Musicæ humanæ tàm ex parte animæ quàm corporis delineatio.

Dies Microcosmicus.

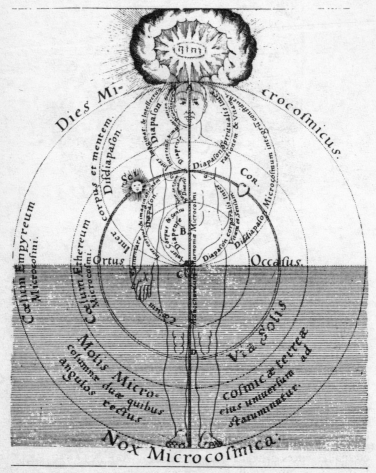

II

16

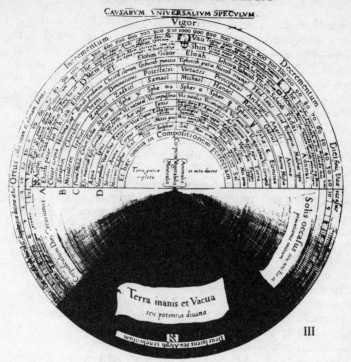

III

RITUAL AND COSMOLOGY

In ritual, everything has an eternal meaning, a purpose. That purpose is to point toward our existence as a microcosm, as a mirror of existence. Hence magic can never be divorced from ritual, though it transcends it, for in ritual alone are the eternal forms purely manifested.

To examine the relation of ritual to the realm of eternal forms, we turn first to Plato's *Timaeus*. In the *Timaeus*, it is said that all things were created eternal, insofar as was possible. And around those eternal essences circulated the temporal, physical images of eternity. All exists according to numbers, and Pythagorean harmony, in and through the higher realm from which it emanates. Hence in Plato we see an immense harmonic cosmos, a revolving wheel of time circling round the eternal essences of which it is a reflection. And in Eternity, said Plato, 'was' and 'will be' – past and future – cannot be

17

attributed to the essences, for as Dōgen said, there is only 'is.'

Here once again, we see the traditional three-world cosmology. There is the world of images – earth – above which is the realm of the planets, and then that of Essences, above which is the Creator, the Sun of existence, in which all is manifested, from which all arose, and in which it subsides. In the West, as in the East, the mandalic form is the manifestation of the nature of existence as emanation, as union. It is metaphysical, not psychological.

Ritual is related to this mandalic form in that, like it, ritual is the visual physical union of the Sun and matter. But whereas the mandala is a two-dimensional and relatively static representation of the interpenetration of the three worlds – Ideal, Mediate, and Material – ritual is a three-dimensional and active manifestation of the three worlds as one in the Eternal Instant.

For this reason ritual is at the center of all magic and religion. But the true nature of ritual must be wholly and completely understood, for its value and efficacy depend upon the degree of understanding with which it is performed, just as the growth of a tree depends upon its supply of water and soil. In a sense, one could say that through contact with the water of understanding in the soil of existence does the tree of completed Form rise toward the Sun of Reality.

Ritual in magic differs from ritual in religion in that the former is more dynamic, more individualized. Magic is solitary; religion is communal. But, finally, the two are inseparable. Although outwardly the two seem at odds, particularly in the West, they draw upon the same source, the same divine hierarchy. From the Hermeticism of Pico della Mirandola to the Kabbalism of Isaac Luria,[5] from the magic of Agrippa to the daimons of Ficino, all are drawn from and very much a source of life for the Judaic and Christian orthodoxy, just as in China the Taoist orthodoxy was invigorated by the influx of unorthodox, or black magicians – for to counter them the orthodox were forced to learn their technique.[6] The influx of unorthodox magic in Taoism forced the orthodox Taoist priests to renew their contact with the celestial, daimonic (or angelic) realm, creating a new and more powerful magic of their own called Thunder Magic, so that they were not rendered powerless – mere vessels devoid of water – before the more innovative and daring unorthodox local magicians.

18

In a sense, one could say that magic is the water and religion is the soil. The two are sterile without that which binds and exalts them: the Tree of ritual. In a tree, we see all four elements united in harmony: air water, soil and fire – that is, life, or sun. They join to form a fifth element: wood, the *quinta essentia*. If one of the other elements is missing, the wood – the tree – dies. A perfect equilibrium in the tree, as in ritual, must be maintained. The tree, as ritual, is the manifestation of the seed of thought, or intent. Both grow and are realized through the perfect pattern provided by the remembrance of and adherence to the celestial realm.

In ritual, then, as in a tree, all four elements are combined to form a fifth: the quintessence. In the same way alchemy is, and must be seen as, ritual. It is not the inept predecessor to modern chemistry, as many would have it, any more than Zodiacal symbolism is the childish precursor of omniscient modern astronomy. Chemistry and astronomy, as externalist sciences, look only at the surface measurements and observations, writing much but saying little, ignoring meaning, and so cannot be confused with the vertically oriented magic and alchemy.

Magic and alchemy are different facets of the same process, the same transformation. Both include elements of herbalism, astrology, minerology, pharmacology, literature, mythology, and many other aspects of human life – under the aegis of ritual – not because magic and alchemy are the primitive precursors of these modern divisions of knowledge, but rather because the essence of magic and alchemy is unification, and above all unification of the three realms. The modern division of science into ever smaller areas of specialization is no sign of progress, for a divided and specialized science can do nothing for the exaltation of man, but rather induces disorder despite its best efforts – disorder of which radioactivity and cancer are but sign and seal. The purpose of magic and alchemy, on the other hand, is to return man to his true position in the center of the cosmos, as microcosm and magician. Hence alchemy and magic naturally encompass all lesser disciplines toward a higher goal: the realization of inherent divinity. To do so requires both exoteric and esoteric knowledge, for the magus must be able to recognize the proper herbs, minerals, conjunctions of stars and planets, as well as the geomantically correct site and the proper correspondences with the human body. The relationship between microcosm and macrocosm is not a metaphor, but a description of reality. As long as science continues to ignore the unifying factor of exalting which conjoins the spheres it will continue to break down into smaller and more specialized disciplines, having an ever more negative effect upon the microcosm – and so upon the world.

The Zen Buddhist monk, Thich Nhat Hanh, when he began his Zen training, could not understand the reason why the Master demanded that he place his shoes correctly before entering the zendo, or why he should eat, sleep and act according to very ritualized movements, for this seemed very much at odds with his Zen training,[7] which was supposed, he thought, to lead to utter freedom, enlightenment, and liberation. It was many years, he wrote, before he realized that it was in this very ritual of taking off the shoes and placing them, for instance, that enlightenment was manifested. Zen, he said, is the realization of the Buddhanature in the most common elements of daily life, raising them to the level of ritual, a manifestation of the transcendent Sun. Zen is none other than here and now.

Alchemy and magic, while leading toward this exaltation and unification of daily life, seldom reach this level. Rather, in alchemy and in magic, all life is compressed into one short span and a selected space through a very specialized and perfected ritual, in which the Eternal is realized. Moreover, the ritual is oriented, nominally at least, toward an end: in alchemy, the end is the creation of the Elixir of Life; in magic the end is the casting out or pacification of the lower demons in favor of the angelic higher daimons. In both of these, however, if the alchemist or magician thinks that anything he does is other than the transformation of his mind and the consequent realization of Mind, he is sadly mistaken. In Renaissance England, those who took alchemy only literally were known as 'puffers' and were scorned by men like Paracelsus and Kelly who, while not denying the actual transmutation of base matter into gold, recognized that there are levels of gold – a symbolic hierarchy – and that without acquisition of the two higher levels, which in Paracelsus's terms were etheric and then heavenly gold, the grosser material alchemy was impossible.

The 'puffers' were those with great laboratories and constantly puffing bellows, but no inner knowledge: it is they who were the precursors of modern chemistry. It is of course an ironic paradox that, were the puffers to have realized the two higher, inner forms of gold, that very spiritual struggle would have annihilated the urge to pile up gold on the material level. Either way, poverty awaited them.

Alchemy and magic, then, are alike in that they share the characteristic of compressed, limited rituals, with their aim the exaltation and purification of the magus. But, like the Zen Buddhist at all times, within those rituals the magus must maintain absolute awareness and consciousness of every action and thought down to the most minute level. The ritual is the focussing of absolute awareness upon a finite place and time: it is the conjunction of the Sun of knowledge with the Moon of mercurial breath and matter within a vessel, an alembic, a magic circle.

For this reason, every object, thought, movement and word of a ritual has immense significance. With the magician, this heightened awareness begins with the drawings of the magic circle. The circle is drawn to signify the infinity of the spheres, the circle being endless, perfect. Within the circle there is either – or both – a cross and a square. The cross and the square, being two right angles, are different forms of the same symbol: two right angles joined at their apex form a cross; two right angles joined at their tips form a square. Both symbolize the earth, and matter. They ground the ceremony, so to speak, as a reminder of the essential unity of the three worlds. The cross symbolizes the four directions, as does the square. The square also implies the diamond shape – the vajra. The diamond is important in that it is clear and yet holds within it all colours, it scratches and yet cannot be scratched – and it is the ultimate product of a very long process of compression and purification. Hence at the beginning of the ritual, both infinity and the diamond are already there, but uncharged, unrealized. In the beginning is contained the end, as the seed contains the tree.

In Tibetan Tantrism, when the square is placed outside the circle, it symbolizes the womb, and the ascendence of the mercurial breath. When the square is placed inside the circle, on the other hand, it symbolizes the vajra, and the ascendence of the sulphurous, flaring knowledge. In either case, when a square is placed upon the cross of four directions, an eight-pointed figure is created; the cardinal directions, by halves, are then invoked into the microcosm of the magus in their center. Each direction corresponds to a colour, and to a particular organ within the body of the magus, as well as to specified parts of his hands, his head, and his solar plexus.[8] In the same way, in Taoism and Tantrism – as in European magic[9] – mudras, or ritual hand movements, are necessary to invoke the spirits, as another reminder of the unity of microcosm and macrocosm.

The spirits are exteriorizations of Mind, made manifest through the heightened awareness of ritual. After any ritual, the spirits are laid to rest, so that Mind is clearer after the ritual than before, much as the bodhisattva Majusri dispels ignorance and cuts away desire with the sword of knowledge and compassion, in order that all beings be liberated. The magus is, by virtue of his ritual, entrusted with much the same task: the pacification and enlightenment of all beings. So great a responsibility necessarily demands that the magus undertake every aspect of the ritual with immense care.

So, in Taoist magic, the ritual even includes the position of the magician's teeth: they are to be held four together on the right, then four together in the front, and finally four together on the left, or in the reverse order. This is to remember the eight directions by meeting four teeth with four teeth, as well as to recall the twelve signs of the Zodiac (3×4). In ritual, even so apparently meaningless a detail as meeting the teeth together, then, assumes the immense value of signifying the union of time – the Zodiac – and space – the eight directions – within the microcosm, the magus.

Almost always, in ritual – Eastern or Western – a sword or dagger is used, particularly to draw the circle that protects and designates the ritual area. The sword is used for several reasons. The sword, having two edges, implies duality – the cause and effect, the phenomenal polarity of existence. Yet the two edges are joined in a single point, much as mind is concentrated and made aware in ritual. The purpose of meditation is the very onepointedness, a onepointedness which, like the sword, is a means of vanquishing one's inner enemies – ignorance, sloth, envy, duality and desire – all of which are manifestations of ego, of the illusory separation of I and thou. Another word for ego is habit, and it is this habit energy that the sword dispels, that Mind might arise.

A square is drawn within the circle by the *arthame*, or magic sword, in order to signify the alchemical paradox, the squaring of the circle – the product of which, mathematically, is a transfinite number, a sign of the infinite celestial realm with which the ritual implicitly begins, and with which it ends, having been realized.

Traditionally, other ritual implements associated with magic are the bell, the book, and the candle – with good reason. The bell signifies the union of the lingam and the yoni, the Sun and Moon, through the union of the handle with the bell itself. The sound which they make when united is Eternal, the manifestation of Mind itself, wholly pure and clear. The use of the bell in ceremony – as a sound which penetrates all the spheres – is common not only in Oriental, but Occidental ritual as well. As late as 1730, the instructions for the creation of a ritual bell were being circulated in France, as testified to by the manuscript by Girardius entitled 'Clochette magique et son usage' which details the specifics of the bell's construction.[10]

On the bell the characters or symbols of the planets are to be inscribed, above which is the Tetragrammaton, and the words ADONAI and IESUS. Like the Tibetan bell which unifies the womb and the vajra, the European bell also symbolized the union and interpenetration of the three worlds. The metals with which the bell was constructed symbolize the lowest, earthly realm. The signs of the planets symbolize the mundus media, the celestial realm of Plato's 'governors', as well as the stages of the spiritual journey. The Hebrew characters of the Tetragrammaton, the Highest Name of God, symbolize and invoke the Mind from which all emanates and in which all has its existence. ADONAI and IESUS symbolize the two aspects of Mind, knowledge and compassion, also the two central aspects of the Buddhanature. The bell is also part of the Western tradition in that it draws upon the Pythagorean teaching that all existence is based upon harmonic structure, and so when the proper chord is struck, it reverberates throughout the cosmos, a concept precisely aligned with the Tibetan esoteric teaching.[11]

In the book, of course, we see the sacred scripture, the mantra or invocation of the eternal realm of essences, and of Mind. All letters contain a numerical equivalent or counterpart which suggests their correlation to the harmonic patterns which underlie and in fact create the cosmos, so that sacred syllables and letters, or *bija* (Sanskrit) derive directly from the higher celestial realm, and manifest aspects of it. Hebrew, Arabic, and Greek, all sacred languages, partake of this number to letter symbolism, and in each of the languages the interpretation of the esoteric meaning of the scriptures hinges upon their elucidation through *gematria*.[12] In the Indo-European, as opposed to the ideographic languages of the East, the consonants provide the form and exoteric meaning, while the vowels contain the spirit, the soul of the language, and in this way, as through the hidden number system, the celestial world is visible in human language.

Hence in the Nag Hammadi Library, the most recent collection of Gnostic Christian writings, we find long strings of vowels: aaaaeeeeiiiioooouuuu. Likewise, in the Tibetan *mantras*, we find that vowels predominate, because they are the invocation of the spirit, not the outer shell of ordinary language. Perhaps there, in part, lies the meaning of the enigmatic letters preceding each Qu'ranic chapter.

But in another sense, the sacred book in ritual provides the form: for the written word is also a vessel, in which the form of a ritual can be maintained throughout the centuries, so that the same ritual may be performed 2,000 or 3,000 years later, awaiting only the human spirit with which it must be fulfilled, and which it fulfills. Without the book, tradition easily degenerates and disappears. With it, though, tradition can become rigid, ossified, dogmatic, sterile and stagnant. The mantra is the bridge between these extremes: it is the spirit in transmissible form.

The candle, too, is of great significance, in that it is a microcosm of the entire ritual, and of its eventual end: purification and transformation. The yellow of tallow – earth – and the white of water are conjoined in its base, for its material substance is oily, dense and waxy, symbolic of our corporeal life. It implies the Platonic, or Plotinian entrapment in matter, in the darkness and ignorance of the soul who has fallen to earth, lost her wings and become blind. Above the white and yellow of water and earth is the flame which purifies the dross below. The flame is lit by awareness, by meditation concentrated upon the ritual Eternal Now. As it burns, it consumes the dross of ignorance and the bonds of entrapment in matter below, creating of it pure radiant bliss, and light. From below, seeing the black smoke and feeling the heat, the 'matter' sees the flame as wrath, burning it unjustly. Yet from above, from the light, the flame is seen for what it is – compassion, freedom, and enlightenment. Divine wrath and Divine compassion are the same thing seen from opposite sides. In the West, wrath tended to prevail; in the East, compassion. This is true exoterically and esoterically, for to be oriented to the rising Sun has great inner significance. At the end of the wholly complete spiritual journey, the Sun is said to rise in the West – that is to say, the Poles unite, and a wholly new Day begins.[13]

Continuing the imagery of the candle: at the base is the square of earth, then the circle of water, the triangle of flame, the semicircle of black smoke, and then, finally, the blue semicircle joined to a triangle of pure light. Above the red triangle of flame, then, is the black semicircle of smoke, above which is the transcendent unity of the light – blue, ether. When the highest – blue – is joined to the lowest – yellow – and earth, then green, the merger of the two and the colour of the living world develops. The colours are yellow which passes into red, and then into blue, so that when the transformation is complete, the emerald or jade stone of Knowledge which lies at the top of Mount Sumeru, the center of the cosmos, is seen. Passing through the visionary colours, one recapitulates the creation of existence.

Incense, as well as certain mild foods, may be used in ritual – in conjunction with bell and candle – in order to symbolize and reinforce the transmutation of the ordinary senses into transcendent senses. With the conquering and rechanneling of habit energy, with the transcendence of the illusory ego, one begins to experience celestial scents, celestial sounds, celestial colours. The incense, candle, bell and other ritual devices both evoke and manifest the celestial senses. These celestial senses include the perception of extremely intense colours – particularly the colours mentioned above – astonishingly loud sounds, as the prevalence of vajra, or thunder magic worldwide would indicate, and intoxicating scents. They may also include an intense heat generated from below the diaphragm, in what Taoists call the 'Court of the Yellow Emperor.' In Tibet this heat forms the basis of a fire yoga, the heat from the practice of which allows the Tibetans to live comfortably in incredibly cold circumstances, often with virtually no clothing – and allows the ritual Alexandra David-Neel describes, of jumping in an iced-over river, nude, and allowing sheets dipped in the icewater to be placed on one's back, sheets which the Tibetans dry with the heat of fire yoga.[14]

Although the origin of these phenomena – celestial sounds, sights, and heat – might appear inexplicable, unreachable, it is not. For as we have seen, the purpose of ritual is to amplify the magus as microcosm. This amplification, paradoxically, relies upon the 'dropping away,' or transcendence of the magician's habit energy and ego, and the consequent intense awareness which is produced.[15] If habit energy, which forms a kind of barrier or filter around us, is transcended, or 'drops away' as we 'rise', then our senses will begin to receive an amplified vision of the world – they will begin to receive purer and clearer perceptions of the world as it is, a reflection of the celestial essences. In Platonic or Hermetic terms, the senses will begin to apprehend the realm of celestial forms and images, closely related to the Buddhist Pure Land, or the Persian Hurqūlyā, the celestial realm. This realm, which contains the essence of material phenomena, is in fact inseparable from those phenomena, which are its reflection. The perception of that realm is what Jacob Böehme meant by 'the signature of all things.' The Gnostics and Hermetic philosophers expressed this in mythological terms as the resurrection of the divine Sophia, or soul, which, after passing over the sea of matter, seeing her own reflection and being attracted downward, must be raised up from that sea in which she is entrapped.

The appearance of celestial senses – celestial sights and sounds – in primordial ritual signifies that the journey back toward the Source is beginning; it signifies that habit energy is transcended, and truer sights and sounds are manifesting, which Böehme called the 'play of the angels in the sight of God.'[16] But as Böehme reiterated, one must never cling to such sounds or sights. In the highest sense, as Zen Buddhism maintains, these manifestations are nothing more than *makyo*, or illusion. For the purpose and meaning of ritual is to be found in the transcendence of both Form and Formless, in the ascent 'above' temporality and ego, so that Mind may be wholly manifested. In Taoism, this point is termed *wu wei*, and refers to a state in which one is like a moon shining upon a calm, limpid lake. In Renaissance alchemy, this state is seen as the final purification of the prima materia, and its transmutation into the philosopher's stone which transmutes and exalts all it encounters. To the extent that this state of *wu wei*, of transcendence, is reached is the magic or alchemical ritual rite successful.

It is to this awareness of the inner unity and sympathetic correspondence of all things – of their Origin – that the magic and alchemical ritual correspondence – tables of herbs, planets, minerals and animals – are meant to point. To the extent that one realizes their meaning are the tables of value, and yet, paradoxically, as one approaches the realization of the philosopher's stone they become mere appurtenances, inferior to the awareness of Mind which reveals the deepest signatures of all things.

Ritual begins with the magus acting as host, host to the guests which he invokes. But those spirits which he invokes are in fact aspects of his own inherent Mind and as they are exteriorized, manifested, he recognizes them as aspects of Mind – that is, they are seen to have as much or more 'reality' than the magus himself. This can be seen in the Tantric visualization practice, in which the Tantrist virtually creates the inner vision of the bodhisattva, down to the minutest detail, in order to recognize that aspect of himself as Mind. In Taoist magic,[17] as in European, the key is to be familiar with the forms and features, the characteristics of that daimon, or celestial being, for without that familiarity, one cannot summon – or visualize – it. Hence most magicians guard the exact features of those beings with whom they are familiar, for it is in those details that their power resides.

Through the ritual these beings take on a kind of material – and very real – existence by virtue of the heightened awareness and concentration of the magus. Through ritual, Alexandra David-Neel once created, during her years in Tibet, a small, roundfaced monk who accompanied her about, was greeted as a real person by others, and finally began to become an independent being out of her control, so that she had to dissolve him, with great effort. This story carries within it the implicit danger of ritual visualization, for the ritual changes the very nature of one's relationship with the celestial world – either for the better, or for the worse. At the beginning of the ritual, one is host – as was Alexandra David-Neel to her little

27

monk. But through the nature of ritual, one eventually becomes guest and the 'visualization' is found to have, in Reality, as much or more 'existence' than oneself, be it Divine or otherwise.

In the beginning of ritual, ego is host. At the end of a primordial ritual, ego is seen to be the illusory guest, subsumed to the celestial realities. In this lies the fundamental difference between modern — especially behavioral — psychologies and traditional magic and alchemy. For in nearly all modern psychological models the ego is given a preeminent place — the 'goal' is not transcendence, but merely establishing a kind of balance in which ego is always host. Even the Jungian psychological model posits the 'archetypes', which are the closest modern concept to that of the celestial realm, in the 'collective unconscious' — that is to say *below* the conscious mind rather than above it. In other words, nearly all modern psychological systems posit the inversion of the traditional triadic hierarchy — in which the celestial beings are *above* the merely mortal ego, and in fact have more reality than the ego — suggesting instead that all must be subsumed to the realm of dualistic phenomena, of ego. The most outlandish example of this tendency is to be found in that which is called 'behaviorism', in which nothing but the grossest physical causes and effects are recognized. In brief, one could well say that while the bulk of modern psychological systems exalt — and condemn — ego, in primordiality, it is transcended. In all traditional teachings, ego is recognized as, at best, a guest of the host: Mind.

The 'psychism' and 'neoshamanism' of the present era are but 'extensions' of the same inversion of the primordial glimpsed in modern psychology — in which the manipulative ego seeks to 'rule' the celestial, and in so doing becomes instead ruled by the infernal, much as Alexandra David-Neel was threatened by her 'monk.' In brief, the same polarity of which we have spoken before obtains in ritual visualization — if the visualization is of the Divine, enclosed within tradition, then one 'ascends' and radiates beneficence. But if the visualization is, inversely, governed by ego, outside tradition — then one 'descends' and is overwhelmed, destroyed by the infernal and malignant. The tree is known by its fruit.

And with that we conclude, turning to some specific elements of ritual: to ritual gesture and posture in the primordial world.

ON RITUAL GESTURE AND POSTURE

One of the most startling things about the study of magic and alchemy is the revelation of its worldwide unanimity in both ritual form and traditional cosmology. There is almost always a ritual sword, a ritual circle, a hierarchy of spirits ascending from those below – earth, air, fire and water – through the intermediate realms and the stellar daimons, to the inexpressible, Mind. There are always planetary symbols and correspondences, amulets, and certain kinds of spells. It should not be surprising, then, that the Western magicians develop a ritual system of gestures for invocation just as their counterparts in China, Japan and Tibet have done. Indeed, the Oriental forms of ritual hand positions are so widespread that every statue, image and icon can be seen to be forming its given *mudra*, one reason for which is that inasmuch as the *mudra* can be formed by anyone, so too the Buddhanature which it expresses is inherent within them. But in the West, due in large part to the eventual separation of religion and magic and the consequent lack of direct transmission of esoteric teaching within a unified system, ritual hand positions are much less widely known. Nonetheless, they did exist.

However, since the philosophic and cosmological structure upon which alchemy and magic is based is so little understood in the modern world, no one has, to my knowledge, either noticed or commented upon the use of ritual hand movements and positions in European magical texts. In fact, the use of *mudras* in even Eastern texts has been largely overlooked, not least because the transmission of their meaning is only oral, and therefore even when ritual texts depicting the hand positions have been smuggled to the West, their significance is in general unknown, rendering them obscure and useless. One such text was obtained from a young novice priest in the Shingōn sect in Japan, and published in France in the late nineteenth century, even though it had been closely guarded prior to that. Despite its publication, its meaning remains obscure, needless to say, for transmission can only occur within a tradition.

And the ritual hand positions used in the West – and their esoteric meaning – are even more obscure, since there has never been a continuous, direct transmission of knowledge in Europe in the way that it took place in, for instance, Tibet, where spiritual alchemy was retained as the essence and lifeblood of religious life, being as it is the individual contact with the Divine. In Tibet, the *lamas*, while maintaining a communal religious life united in ritual, nonetheless live alone in scattered quarters, where their magic and their inner alchemical trans-mutations take place in solitude and for which they are accountable only to their *guru*.[18]

But even though the specific uses and meanings of ritual hand movements have been eclipsed in the Western world, the continuation of particular gestures in society bespeaks their nature as manifestations of the Eternal, for they are still invested with some unknown power. One, for instance, is still feared in Italy today as a magic gesture: the *mano cornuta*, or horned hand. It is formed by extending the little finger and the index finger, holding the thumb over the other two, creating the image of the Bull, symbol of virility, fertility, and generative strength. The sign is interpreted, in Italian folklore, as either striking a woman barren, or allowing her impregnation, and is commonly assumed to be still used by witches there.

Another such gesture is the extended middle finger which, termed the 'bird' in American slang, is a sign of disrespect and hostility. Clearly phallic, it, like the *mano cornuta*, is the manifestation of will and masculinity, and hence is character-istic of both Italy and the United States, both countries which tend to adopt exaggeratedly masculine stereotypes. As signs of power, both were used in magic ritual in order to subdue demons, the projections of ego, and to direct spirits of lower nature. It seems evident, then, why these signs survived, given their associations with masculinity and their purpose in the direction of the infernal realm. The phallic sign is close in nature to the sign of the sacred sword – the index and middle fingers extended, the thumb across the other two bent fingers' nails. In Taoist magic, this sign is used to direct, to channel spirits in manifestation,[19] but it can be seen in European manuscripts as well.

One sign with a deeper meaning which has also survived is that of a fist with the thumb protruding between the index finger and the middle finger. Surviving as an obscene gesture simulating copulation, the sign is also found in magical manuscripts, where its significance is left unstated. One such instance is reprinted below. But from the obvious sexual connotations, the sign must be closely aligned with the *vajra* mudra found in Tibetan tantrism, a sign which signifies the interpenetration of the womb and the diamond realms – the male Intellect[20] penetrating into the Womb of Reality. Clearly the symbolism surrounding the vajra mudra is greater than that of the European gesture: the *vajra* includes much of the symbolism of the *stupa* mentioned earlier, embodying the square, the circle, the triangle, and the semicircle-triangle, marked by the index finger of the left hand, as well as the interpenetration of the realms. In the European sign, the thumb separates the index from the other three fingers, symbolizing the union of the Trinity of eternal principles into One. In addition, the sign suggests the Orphic Egg,[21] the thumb being the flow of the Divine, as well as the escape of the Fish from the Net.[22] Finally, like the *vajra* mudra, it must be seen to imply the interpenetration of the phenomenal world and Reality.

One other gesture which has been retained and which has an esoteric aspect is that most common of signs: the index finger touching the thumb, forming a circle, the three fingers, slightly bent, extended outward. Generally acknowledged as meaning that everything is all right, in esoteric terms it signifies the three pillars, or Trinity of alchemical principles – Mercury, Sulphur and Salt – and the Void, the Emptiness from which they arose.

There are, however, a large number of other hand positions that have not been retained, but which can be recovered by examining some of the surviving manuscripts, for just as one can find no Buddha in the East whose hands are not forming an esoteric mudra, so too in the West one can find few authentic pictures of magicians who do not carry encoded in their hands one or another esoteric gesture. In Agrippa's monumental *de Occulta Philosophia*, Chapter XVI, Book II, p. CXXXIX is devoted to the esoteric gestures of antiquity which expressed numbers, and when one recalls the Pythagorean teaching of harmonics, and the idea that numbers and harmonic proportions determine the nature and existence of all things, it is not surprising that the magician would teach that the human body itself echoes these proportions and numbers. For since the Western tradition tends to emphasize the mathematical harmony of the macrocosm, it is only natural that the individual magus draws upon the numerical harmony in the microcosm. Thus Agrippa said that the left hand, when turned backward on the chest, fingers upward, signified 10,000, while the left hand grasping the left thigh signified 60,000. That Agrippa was not alone, but rather part of a great tradition, can be seen in a codex in the Nationalbibliotek in Vienna. In this beautifully illustrated manuscript, one of several devoted to ritual hand gestures still extant, we see not only the gestures which are related to given numbers, but below the depicted gestures, we see the magus himself with his hands clasped over his head, forming the eternal circle from which all emanates, while beside him is the bear, associated with Ursa Major in both East and West. Ursa Major is a pivotal constellation in all magic ritual in that it is circumpolar – it never sets – and it points, as it rotates, to the Gate of Life.[23] In the succeeding pages of illustrated text we see the ritual hand positions associated with particular constellations which are marked within the depicted scorpion, bull, and so on, in order that they can be recognized in the night sky.

Hence in the West there is a tradition of esoteric hand positions much like those reproduced, from the Shingōn sect of Japanese Buddhism. On the other hand, as noted before, this is not to imply that every culture is identical, nor that there has been contact between cultures, but rather that esoteric hand positions are a natural means of expressing aspects of Reality and so must recur within every culture, varying with cultural features. And so while Oriental gestures tend to depict particular characteristics of given bodhisattvas, Western gestures tend to express mathematical expressions, due in large part to the Pythagorean and Platonic origins of Western thought. In fact, there are strong suggestions that Greek, like Hebrew, is a language which bears within it a universal language based upon geometrical and numerical meanings, so that much Greek architecture, for instance, bears encoded within it measurements the Divine Reality as personified in the form of the gods, which are in fact harmonic principles.[24] These principles can be revealed by the conversion of letters into numbers, and numbers into letters, a science termed *gematria*.

Again, the reason that geometrical and numerical forms hidden in language are important is that, as Plato – and the Hermetic tradition in general – asserts, the closer one approaches the Divine, the more one approaches the realms of geometric harmony and perfection, the realm of Pure Form of which this world is but an imperfect reflection upon matter. Since the human being is intended to be the Pole and the microcosm in which the three worlds of matter, Form and Reality meet, it is natural that the human body should mirror that higher Reality. This is the reason the Hermetic writers continually place the human body within geometric designs, as seen in the illustrations in the works of Henry Cornelius Agrippa,[25] for since both the cosmos and the human microcosm are patterned upon divine harmonies and geometric Form, by forming *mudras* which manifest this harmony the magus is at once recognizing and realizing those Divine Forms of which he, like the cosmos, is a reflection, an image. The images formed by the hands, like the human body itself, are a recognition of that which lies beyond the transient temporal world.

In these diagrams of the human body superimposed upon celestial Form, and, significantly, upon the star or pentagram, we can see the higher origins of the hand gestures and postures. For the gestures and postures are formed to invoke those Divine aspects seen in the microcosm – man. So we see in both Western manuscripts and Taoist magic texts the reiteration of cosmic symbolism not only upon the body, but upon the hand as well. In Taoism, the hand positions are often related to the square of Saturn superimposed upon the hand, as below. In invoking particular star daimons or earth spirits, certain points are pressed on this diagram, both as a means of remembering and of manifesting the celestial origins of the magus himself. This is a large part of the secret of magic squares – and of most esoteric diagrams – for they are themselves an expression of celestial harmony and proportion, but acquire their power only upon their use in ritual, in physical manifestation. The Taoist hand gestures and diagrams are mirrored in Agrippa and Fludd's hand diagrams, patterned after Zodiacal symbolism, for despite ill-informed suggestions to the contrary, these diagrams are not for use in chiromancy, or mere deterministic fortune telling, but rather like astrology, are the manifestation of Divine principles which the magus invokes and realizes through ritual. Taoists, significantly, often use the square of Saturn as the basis for ritual dance steps as well, for the essence of magic lies in the manifestation of the celestial in the physical in every possible way, in order to reveal the Divine Forms behind transient phenomena, and it is this that ritual gesture and posture most immediately does.

Esoteric postures, however, are intended not so much as a means of reflecting the Divine, but rather as a stabilizing position which allows the mind to become clear, and habit energy to 'break down.' One of those postures is of course the traditional lotus position, a position which folds the legs in, seating one on three points – the knees and buttocks – and which holds one in a state of concentrative tension. Although this posture is shown in both ancient Mayan and ancient Egyptian temple illustrations, it is not, to my knowledge, found in the West. Rather, the traditional Western position, as seen in manuscripts depicting alchemists and magicians, is to kneel with the back straight, the hands folded palm to palm in a gesture of obeisance to Mind. More important than the actual position, though, is the perseverance with which the ritual meditation is approached. As John Aubrey said of a gentleman who conversed with Angels and Spirits 'his knees did become horny from praying,' so must all who would rise toward the celestial realm meditate with that intensity. Zen Master Dōgen, it was said, would carry his sitting cushion with him wherever he went, constantly seeking to do zazen until his legs fell off. To conquer the bonds of time and matter requires superhuman perseverance. In both Western and Eastern ritual, it is not uncommon to meditate with a candle atop one's head. It is said in the Shingōn sect of Buddhism that one should be unaware that the candle has gone out due to the depth of one's *samadhi*, or meditative absorption.

And, properly, it is with this aspect of ritual gesture and posture that one must conclude. For neither magic nor religion can become alive and take on true meaning without the direct apprehension of Reality, and that experience can only begin with the struggle against habit energy and ego as encountered in silence and ritual meditation. From the writings of the ancient Taoist to the teaching of Zen Master Dōgen, this above all in emphasized. Indeed, the diagrams and ritual gestures are but a gloss pointing toward the heart of both magic and religion: the individual experience of the Divine Reality. Ritual is intended, above all, to develop Awareness, Awareness of the Divine and Awareness of the significance of every action, every aspect of the body and of movement. But this Awareness cannot flower without constant ritual meditation. The purpose of ritual gesture and posture – as manifested through tradition – is to realize, in every sense of the word, that which is latent in man as a divine being.

IV   Diagram of the hand, from Agrippa's *de Occulta Philosophia*

NATURAL CORRESPONDENCE

As noted earlier, sympathetic action, or natural correspondence, is a central element of the practice of magic, for it is the recognition of the mediate realm of the three spheres, and a natural manifestation of the realization of the unity underlying diversity. Natural correspondence is nothing less than a means of relating all phenomena to their higher, celestial Forms by

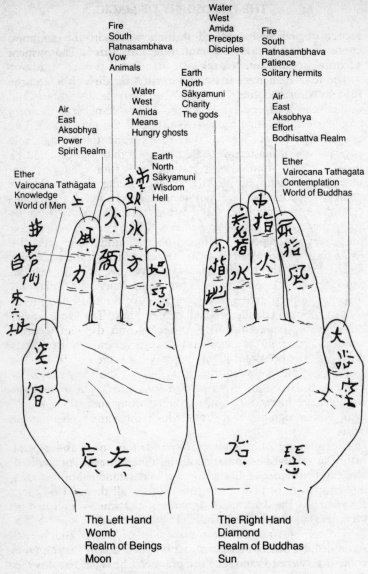

Fire
South
Ratnasambhava
Vow
Animals

Water
West
Amida
Means
Hungry ghosts

Air
East
Aksobhya
Power
Spirit Realm

Earth
North
Sākyamuni
Wisdom
Hell

Ether
Vairocana Tathāgata
Knowledge
World of Men

Water
West
Amida
Precepts
Disciples

Earth
North
Sākyamuni
Charity
The gods

Fire
South
Ratnasambhava
Patience
Solitary hermits

Air
East
Aksobhya
Effort
Bodhisattva Realm

Ether
Vairocana Tathagata
Contemplation
World of Buddhas

The Left Hand
Womb
Realm of Beings
Moon

The Right Hand
Diamond
Realm of Buddhas
Sun

(Adapted from Rambach, *Tantric Buddhism*)

V   Symbolism of the fingers according to a Buddhist model.
Note the parallelism of right and left, Sun and Moon

36

recognizing their essence, and their place on the temporal spectrum. The best known means of doing this is arrangement according to the four elements.

The four elements correspond to the four directions and the four outstretched limbs of man, and provide a constant and unified means of understanding the origins of natural phenomena, perfectly relating the macrocosm and the microcosm. The ancients did not regard the four elements as the sole constituents of matter; they did not teach that matter could be broken down into these. Rather, the four divisions are principles, means of identifying and seeing the origins of natural phenomena. The four elements were never the predecessors of the periodic table, which divides nature into its component parts. The four elements unify. For this reason, on the diagrams reprinted from Robert Fludd, one sees the emanation of existence from the Divine, through the cherubim and seraphim, through the planetary divisions, and through the four elements into the world of multiplicity. One diagram useful in understanding the relationship of the four elements is that of the two triangles joined at their apex. The top triangle, point down, represents water, mercury and the female principle; on its right top corner is moisture and on its left is coldness. The bottom triangle, point up, is representative of the male principle, sulphur and fire. Its left bottom corner is dryness and its right bottom corner is heat. When the two triangles are merged, of course, the resulting sign is Solomon's Seal, which signifies that from which the varied phenomena arise.

The teaching of natural correspondences, once the central principle involved is understood, becomes utterly comprehensive, and provides a means for the understanding of the uses and properties of plants, minerals, stars – all things. Consider, for example, the doctrine of signatures, as Paracelsus termed it, in regard to the use of plants. Imagine a man alone in the wilderness, surrounded by a profusion of plants and herbs, some deadly, others beneficent. How could he tell them apart? If the man were to randomly sample them, he would be dead in a matter of days by sheer chance. The solution is to examine the plants according to their signature – that is, according to their resemblance to various functions and parts of the human body. For instance, pitch from a pine tree, being the execrescence of a wound in the tree, provides a good poultice, just as vines, being similar to veins, are probably efficacious in aiding circulation. Yellow plants, closely aligned with the colour of jaundice, are helpful in treating liver ailments, just as plants covered with fine hair are probably of use in treating skin and scalp irritations. There is nothing whatever farfetched about such correspondences: they are simple common sense, drawn from the principle of the essential unity of man and cosmos.

To deny that essential unity is to march firmly toward isolating ourselves and building up the barriers of habit energy which screen us from ourselves and from our world. To relinquish that principle of unity is like the son who squanders his inheritance in the city, ignoring his own royal lineage and wandering forlorn, having forgotten his true place. Having left that royal home, no matter what he accumulates in the city, it will not recompense him for that original loss of unity. Magic and alchemy are none other than steps on that path back to the royal home; natural correspondences are the reflections of that transmutation within the magus. Seeing into one's own origin is to see into that of all phenomena.

But natural correspondence can also aid in that transmutation. Just as the correspondences of the herbs – chosen according to their relation with the human body – can heal physical illness, so the same correspondences, raised to a higher level, can heal the deeper spiritual ills through ritual. Most valuable, then, are those plants which harmonize with the colours and scents of a given realm or aspect of ritual transmutation. Such plants include 'Master of the Woods,' which yields a red dye from its roots and a green dye from its leaves, both colours essential to spiritual alchemy. Similarly, wintergreen and mistletoe are of use in ceremony. Solomon's Seal, the roots of which bear the superimposed triangles, is important in ritual, as are vervain and ferns. Mandrake, because of its humanoid form, is also important, though it must be handled with care, as must the dark plants, like nightshade and henbane, which take their place when one is expelling and laying to rest the wrathful demons. As for the specific uses of specific plants, the best place to begin is the work of Marsilio Ficino and Agrippa, both of whom devote much to the ceremonial herbal.

It is significant that the Sanskrit word from which *Tantra* is drawn is the word for cloth, or weaving, much as the Arabic word from which *Sūfi* is derived means woolen cloak, or woven garment. For it is through the doctrine of signatures, of natural correspondence, that we see the warp and weft of our existence at the center of the cosmos; we are, then, clothed with the priceless garment of original unity when we become wholly aware of the patterns and harmony of the cosmos.

Perhaps the most charming vindication of the path toward regaining the Divine clothing of natural correspondences is to be found in the writings of the Taoists, whose wistful and often fantastic works frequently refer to that aim. One of the best vindications of the teaching of signatures is to be found in Ko Hung's 'Rejoinder to Popular Conceptions,' where he wrote, in response to an anonymous and severe Confucian critic,

> Nobody in creation is cleverer than the human being. Possessed of the most accessible techniques, he can make all creation his servant; having attained the deepest, he can enjoy fullness of life and everlasting vision. Since he knows the best medicines are potent for extending his years, he takes them in his search for geniehood. Knowing the great age attained by tortoises and cranes, he imitates their calisthenics to augment his own lifespan.[26]

In addition, said Ko Hung, 'It is clear that in special areas many creatures far surpass man; this is true not only for the tortoise and the crane.' Accordingly, Ko Hung argued, Fu Hsi wove his nets using spiders for his teachers, just as Shao Hao relied upon the nine quail to determine the seasons, and the Yellow Emperor awaited the cry of the phoenix in order to tune his pitch pipes. Whoever naturally understands these arts may practice them, said Ko Hung. But those who doubt are of course not so destined: there is no point in asking why the ancients were so wise while we ourselves remain ignorant. For, he said, the highest is attainable even yet.

And as to the Confucians who still remain sceptical, Ko Hung fired his parting shot: 'If the people of our day were to call that which they can conceive existent, and that which they cannot conceive nonexistent, then very little would be transpiring in this world of ours.'

It is not, then, by observation of natural phenomena alone

that one becomes a magus, but rather by the attainment of understanding, which is then applied to the natural world, and which can be expressed in terms of tables of correspondence. And, inevitably, the tables of correspondence will be related to the stars and planets.

To understand the relation between the planetary and stellar influences and natural correspondence – and magic itself – one must examine the difference between the modern and the traditional views of astrology. In the modern version of astrology, one's destiny can be described in the motions of the planets and constellations, if one has the skill. According to this view, all is preordained and inflexible; our chief trouble is prediction. While this version of astrology fits in well with the modern horizontal view of existence as progressing from point A to B, it is only half of the meaning of the stars. In the modern view, the stars and planets are seen as external influences which exert control over life, in fact representing *karma*, the accretions of ego which cannot be circumvented, only transcended. Likewise, from the Gnostic perspective, the Zodiac and planets were creations of the demiurge, symbolic of man's entrapment in ego, and his continual recreation of the world in his own image,[27] as opposed to recognizing his true origin in the celestial realm, and transcending the entrapment in ego which the planets and stars symbolized. As a sign of determinism, astrology is a means of seeing the inevitable chains of cause and effect which the ego accumulates.

Yet there is another way to envision the constellations and planets: not as entrapment in the webs of fate and ego, but rather as symbolic of the Divine principles within man through the activation of which one realizes the celestial world. Each of the Zodiacal symbols is, in this traditional view, a complex of esoteric meanings and associations descriptive of aspects of the celestial realm where everything is symbolic, dreamlike. In a sense, one could say that in the former, majority view, the constellations and Zodiacal symbols represent beasts which walk freely in the night of ignorance, and of which most people live in fear, for the beasts seem to have control and to determine their lives.

But in the latter vision, the constellations are illumined and they each assume their proper place within. The beasts and Zodiacal constellations no longer rule, but are ruled, becoming, instead of an obstacle to transcendence, a means towards it.[28] In the common view of astrology, the beasts rule man. In the higher view, man rules the beasts. In the highest vision, all are subsumed in Mind.

And it is upon the higher view that magic and alchemy – and natural correspondence – is based. For in ritual magic, the activation of the constellations through the use of invocations, talismans, times, colour and scent and herb correspondence is nothing other than the activation of principles and aspects within the magus. Of what use, for instance, is knowledge of the melancholic Saturnian influence, if it is not recognized to be the knowledge of something malignant within the magician himself, something to be balanced by light, Jovial and Venusian influences?

This is not, of course, to reduce astrological principles – and natural correspondence itself – to mere psychology, for then it would have no real power. Zodiacal symbolism goes much deeper than that. For inasmuch as everything is a manifestation of Mind, stars have as much external validity as other influences – in fact, they are a universal condensation of those influences. And since we are each none other than Mind, of which those constellations are manifestations, realization of Mind is union with the stars, union with existence itself. It is upon sympathetic harmony, and ultimately upon this realization, that magic ritual depends.

The web of correspondences which centers upon the ritual altar symbolizes the net of existence which one must transcend, and simultaneously is the manifestation of divine unity in the material world before one's very eyes. In the pattern and harmony of the correspondences we see the Mind of which we are and in which alone there is existence. Hence there is another level at which every table of correspondences may be read: as a map of degrees of consciousness or awareness. For example, phenomena might be arranged according to the schema of the production of a diamond. At the lowest level is the *prima materia* – carbon. Cold, black and dead – the detritus of life, the decayed, petrified, base product of existence. Buried deep within the earth, it is subjected to intense pressure and heat, which slowly transforms it into an intermediate form of some hardness and clarity. But if it is subjected to continued heat and pressure, it becomes a diamond – colourless, yet containing all colours. This is also a highly condensed summary of alchemy. But phenomena can – as a rather rough example – be classified according to these levels, relating to the vertical ascent of consciousness.

Consciousness may also be represented on a horizontal scale – and it is here that one finds the forte of most tables of correspondence, which tend to depict aspects, or breadth of consciousness. This is in general the aim of planetary tables, which are used to determine the proper equilibrium of aspects of consciousness, a balance which is necessary if one is to rise – under the proper heat and pressure – to the next highest level on the vertical scale.

We have assumed, here, that tables of correspondence are arranged in the rectangular form, and in general this is the case, this form being useful for depicting phenomena in the temporal world with its four directions. However, another form for tables of correspondence is that of the circle. The circular form was often favored by Renaissance Hermetic philosophers like Robert Fludd, Ramon Lull and Giordano Bruno, all of whom arranged phenomena in memory wheels. The memory wheels were not so much classifications of object – as were the tables – but rather were arrangements of *images*. This is because the memory wheels belong almost wholly to the eternal, celestial realm, whereas the tables belong to the temporal realm. The two are intimately related, are reflections of one another, and are ultimately one and the same. But for the purposes of magic, they must be treated separately. And so the circle, being infinite, contains the images of the celestial realm, while the square contains the vertical levels of consciousness and their horizontal aspects for equilibrium.

For purposes of magic – and to a lesser extent alchemy – the tables are necessary, being related more directly to temporal phenomena. The memory wheels, on the other hand, containing images of the divine realm within man – like 'a huge dark man with burning eyes, carrying a sword'[29] – is used for internal visualization and transmutation. The relation of the wheel to the table is perhaps best understood in light of that ancient Egyptian symbol – the ankh. The ankh is the circle conjoined to the cross below. The circle is the Sun, the Eternal, Divine realm from which all existence emanates. Directly below the circle is the horizontal line of time. Above it is the timeless

42

realm; below it is time, and matter. And emanating from the circle is the vertical, material line of phenomena which becomes denser, more material, and more removed from the Sun the farther down one travels. The ankh is, in fact, not unlike the analogy of the candle, with which it is closely associated in meaning. The area below the timeline in the cross is the area in which the table of correspondence prevails. Above the timeline is Eternity, in which the infinite Wheel is the predominant symbol. In truth, the wheel and the table use the same categorical arrangement and the two realms are ultimately identical – nonetheless, we conceive of them as separate, just as in Buddhism *nirvana* is conceived of as separate from *samsara*, and yet is contained within and interpenetrates it.

Anything found in a genuine table of correspondence – however apparently absurd on a literal level – has its esoteric meaning. For instance, one might read references to the heart of a dove, of a mole, or of a toad. Each of these has an esoteric significance and, like the *Sandyabhasa*, or Sanskrit 'twilight language', is encoded so that several levels of meaning may be invoked at once. When such objects as a mole's heart are called for in a magical or alchemical text, they are to be read most for their inner significance, and least of all literally. The dove symbolizes the *parousia* or Holy Spirit, and the mole the earthbound essence to be transmuted. The toad, living beneath rocks in the damp and cold, symbolizes the very antithesis of the place where one would expect to find the pearl of wisdom, the stone of the philosophers, and it is for that reason that toads and frogs often figure in magic ritual – for it is often said that it is in the toad's mouth that the pearl of wisdom is to be found, meaning that Reality is right here, before us now.

The system of natural correspondences – and its importance in magic and alchemy – itself runs counter to the popular misconception that the magus is *necessarily* in some way evil, for the logical consequence of accepting the unity of all things through natural correspondence is universal compassion. The teaching of natural correspondence implies that everything is interrelated, so that what happens to someone 1,000 miles away, for instance, affects us as well through the interconnectedness of all things. Thus, to the extent that the magus exists within the primordial tradition – in contradistinction to modern 'sorcery' – his action is based upon the recognition of the unity of all things, a realization which nurtures compassion. Even the use of an effigy is a tacit recognition that one is connected intimately with the other regardless of the vastness of time and space – it is a recognition that the two, however distant, are one in Mind.

It is because of the ramifications of natural correspondence – of sympathetic action – that 'black magic' is so inherently self-defeating.[30] That is to say: the magus within the primordial tradition must by definition be purified in consciousness in order to be able to transcend time and space, to manifest the 'Divine affinity.' Thus primordial magic exists at the opposite pole so to speak from 'black magic,' for it implies dropping, cutting down the very attitudes of desire and aversion, greed and hate which motivate the sorceror. In fact, one can well say that the two kinds of magic occupy antithetical historical poles: in the primordial realm magic arises naturally from spiritual ascent and divine affinity; while at the other extreme one finds the descent into the subconscious or infernal realm 'below' ego which characterizes the false mysticism of the 'counter-tradition' and which leads to the dissolution of the false mystic as sorcery necessarily leads to the destruction of the sorceror.

In truth, in our present era it would even be correct to say that that which most people associate with 'black magic' – 'pacts' with demons – is in fact a reflection of the ever deeper modern submersion in ego and in the material realm. 'Everyday life' is in a sense a tacit pact with the demons of desire and aversion. The primordial magician, through ritual, illumines the nature of the demons and lays them to rest, while most people make pacts with the demons by *not* invoking and laying them to rest. For the demons are the projections, the manifestations of ego and habit energy which the magus must mercilessly expel in order that the angelic intelligences may take their rightful place as the manifestation of Mind. And the unity of man and the angelic intelligences are mirrored by the unity of man and the constellations.

For each sign in the Zodiac corresponds to aspects of the cosmic man, and to the magus; by invoking the aspects of the stars, the magus becomes identical with the cosmic man, Adam Kadmon, in the same way that through ritual the Buddhist comes face to face with his own inherent Buddhanature. The most central constellation, though, is the Polar constellation, the Great Bear, Ursa Major.[31] For just as all magic ritual is oriented toward that which never changes, but only revolves – the Pole of existence – so is the ritual oriented toward the outward sign of that Pole: Ursa Major. Ursa Major, which never sets, but only circles Polaris, signifies the wheel of existence, as well as the circle which lies beyond time. In fact, if one takes a timelapse photograph of the northern sky,[32] an extraordinary mandala organized around the eternal center of the north is seen: the sky becomes a whorl around the Pole. But Ursa Major corresponds to the human body itself as well. The four stars arranged in a square signify the four directions, and the basis of all human endeavour – hence they are positioned on the two feet and on the two knees. The upper three stars are placed two inches below the navel (in Zen Buddhism, the *hara*),[33] at the chest, and in the mouth or between the eyes, signifying the three nexus points of consciousness in the human body which correspond to mineral (the base), vegetable (the navel), animal (the chest), and human (the head).

The Taoists call the place at which the three single stars of Ursa Major point the 'gate of life', which corresponds to the crown of the head. The 'gate of life' must be closed – as the focal point of the ritual – before anything else in Taoist ritual can begin.[34] In the *Tibetan Book of the Dead*,[35] this closing of the gate of life is called the 'closing of the womb entrance.' It means, above all, that one can achieve the onepointedness at the beginning of the ritual sufficient to close off extraneous, wandering, thoughts, and allow the formation of a pool of tranquility. This onepointedness is in fact the formation of a kind of inner vessel into which the nectar of celestial union might well. Without closing the gate of life – without onepointedness – the mind is not a vessel, being full of leaks, and nothing in the ritual – nothing of spiritual transmutation – can be accomplished. Ritual – and the use of natural correspondence – are not so much means toward as they are manifestations of this onepointedness, which is in fact the dawning of sight.

Man is not only the measure of all things, he is the mirror of them. The purpose of ritual is to clear that mirror and allow things to reflect in it as they are, to further what is natural. Seeing natural correspondences clearly as the warp and weft of existence is the result of the preliminary cleansing of that mirror. But we are not ony wrapped in the divine clothing of correspondences, we are that cloth. Yet there is a step further, beyond even this realization, and it is to be found in the Zen Buddhist story of the two monks. One was a head monk, in line for the head position in the monastery and, everyone thought, in line for the transmission. The other monk swept floors, and was generally ignored. When the master was about to die, he had the monks demonstrate their Zen. All deferred to the head monk, who wrote the following poem:

> Shining like a mirror
> Not a speck of dust
> No defilement anywhere.

But the other monk crept out during the night and wrote the following lines:

> There is no mirror
> And no dust.
> What is there to be defiled?

The following day that monk received the transmission. For the higher understanding is to see not only the correspondence between forms, the mirror, but to see the essential unity of all Form in Emptiness. That is the truest natural correspondence.

THE WEB OF EXISTENCE

Although we have made passing reference – and shall do so again – to the traditional view of the cosmos as the manifestation of geometric and numerical harmonics, a view which is fundamental to the metaphysics of which magic is a part, it is necessary to dwell more concentratedly upon it, since without some understanding of the mathematical harmony of the spheres and its place in traditional teachings there can be little possibility of realizing the nature of theurgy, of traditional magic.

While this traditional understanding of the cosmos as geometric emanation and harmony has, in the West, been largely relegated to the label 'Pythagoreanism' and thereby often dismissed as simply a peculiar aspect of early Greek philosophy, this understanding ought to be anything but a mere

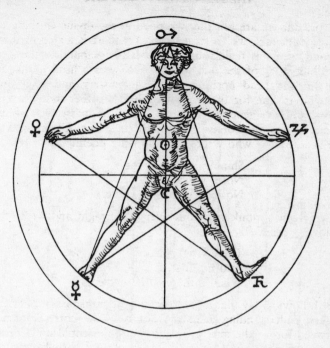

VI   Man as a Celestial being – reproduced from Agrippa's
de Occulta Philosophia

footnote, being in truth fundamental not only to the understanding of Greek teaching,[36] but to the vision of the cosmos
found in every traditional culture, from that of the American
Indian to that of the Taoists in China. And indeed, the
symbolism of numbers and geometry must necessarily be
shared by all traditional cultures, since mathematical harmony
and universality are manifest everywhere, at every glance, if we
have but eyes to see.

In every culture, for instance, four is a revered, essential
number – not arbitrarily so, but rather because the various
manifestations of four are an integral part of the creation, the
pattern of the cosmos. The four directions, the four winds, the
four essential elements of earth, air, fire and water, the four
spirits of stone, thunder, motion and water, the four colours of

VII A Renaissance table of correspondences

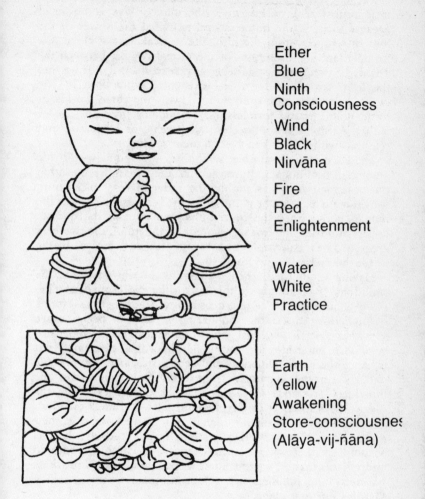

Ether
Blue
Ninth
Consciousness
Wind
Black
Nirvāna

Fire
Red
Enlightenment

Water
White
Practice

Earth
Yellow
Awakening
Store-consciousnes
(Alāya-vij-ñāna)

VIII A Buddhist stupa, each level of which corresponds to one of the
elements, rising from Earth to Fire, Air and Ether

black, red, yellow and white – who can deny their universality, their primal reality? Likewise, the number five is powerful because in it, in the quintessence, is united the power of the four directions within the fifth, the vertical, just as three is a 'completion' or 'resolution' of the primal conflict between the duality of two, and just as seven is powerful since in it we find the four aspects of terrestrial existence, symbolized by the cross,[37] the four directions, united with the three worlds of form, nonform and formlessness of Buddhist metaphysics, or with the three levels of terrestrial, psychic or planetary, and celestial (within *Nous*) of Neoplatonic cosmology.

These aspects of number symbolism are found worldwide among all traditional cultures because they are inherent within the cosmic order – as within the individual as microcosm, something which can be glimpsed in the very architecture of the human body, since the four limbs culminate in the quinate fingers and toes, the five senses unite in the mind, the two eyes are joined by the invisible to make sight (duality resolved by the third, the invisible unity) and so on.

Having established, then, something of the basis for the traditional recognition of the mirrorlike correspondence between man and cosmos microcosm and macrocosm as aspects of numerical emanation and harmony, we can begin to see something of the way in which numerical and geometrical symbolism enter into the traditional philosophy of magic. That is, since the same numerical and geometrical patterns pervade and inform the composition of both the cosmos and the individual, it stands to reason that those changes which the magus seeks to effect in the phenomenal world must take into account a central medium of connection between the two: their mathematical correspondences. But how, precisely, is this accomplished? How are such changes effected? In order to address this matter, we must first reexamine the ways in which geometry and numbers figure in traditional teaching, taking Plato as our first guide.

In the *Timaeus* Plato said that one must above all keep in mind that the four elements – and the physical universe – are not composed of things possessed of any intrinsic nature, but rather all is impermanent, in flux, and consists in changes of *quality*. Thus water is simply that which has the qualities of that liquid, and so forth. Consequently, one must acknowledge that the physical realm, despite its apparent corporeality and solidity, is in truth none other than a 'moving image of "eternity",'[38] to use Plato's own phrase. And the primary way by which we can understand the nature of this 'eternity' is through sign and symbol – that is, through the harmonic order of numbers and words. Hence Plato went on to speak of the Golden Section – those series of numbers culminating in the cube, the symbol of earthly existence $(1, 2, 2^2, 2^3, 3^2, 3^3)$ and of the so-called Platonic solids because with these he was suggesting the nature of the celestial, more eternal, stellar realm of which the flux of the physical world is merely an imperfect reflection. This 'tertiary' level of being is in its very nature by and large inconceivable to us, being accessible to the rational intelligence primarily through the medium of number and geometry, beyond which only the visionary can reach. It is in this 'tertiary' level of the traditional triadic hierarchy of the cosmos that the true magician performs his work, through the 'irradiation' of its beneficent influences. 'Beyond' this is *Nous*, or Mind, or the Reality about which nothing can ultimately be said.[39]

In any case, these celestial, numerical patterns, which are inherent in all things, are closely aligned with the realms of the stars and planets, most principally through the twelve houses of the Zodiac and the seven planets. Traditional cultures, needless to say, display a remarkable similarity as regards astrological symbology precisely because of its universal nature, because through the heavens can be seen most clearly the celestial warp and weft, the mathematical harmonic web of existence.

Magic numbers, magic words, images and the mystery of the planets and stars all are intertwined most intricately, inextricably in the celestial realm, so that the evocation of any one aspect necessarily involves the others. The constellations and the nature of the planetary symbols, for example, are known to us through certain images – such as that of the Lyre, or in the case of the planet Mars, say, that of the Warrior – and yet these are intimately tied to number, form and color in a most subtle way. Incantation, therefore – that is, the evocation of planetary aspects or forces towards a given effect – necessarily involves both numerical and geometrical harmonies, as well as numerically aligned words in a way that can best be demonstrated as below.

We are here using the traditional Western method of sigil formation which, while tacitly Hebrew and Qabalistic, no doubt derived from the Greek and Chaldean, and prior to that, from the Egyptian. Through the ritual use of the sigil the magician calls into play a particular celestial aspect or harmonic level in order to produce a certain effect, or influence. In terms of the Platonic celestial hierarchy discussed earlier, he is 'channeling,' so to speak, the more eternal realm of the Forms in order to alter their 'moving images' or reflections – the phenomenal world.

The magic squares and sigils reproduced in this book come for the most part from Agrippa's *de Occulta Philosophia*, the sigil being the magician's physical manifestation – gestures – in ritual of the geometric harmony within the magic square, which itself bears within it the harmonic essence of, for instance, one of the planets. Though the sigils may vary somewhat from one culture to another, the essential nature of the magic practised – the use of magic words, numbers, signs and planetary influence – remains much the same regardless of its place of origin, be it American Indian, Occidental or Taoist.

The formation of sigils, and their connection with incantory words and numbers, in the Occidental tradition at least, can be seen to have taken place as follows. The magic square of Jupiter, which is a solar planet, can be seen below, as reproduced from Agrippa.[40] Below it is the sigil of the intelligentiae iovis, the geometric sign inscribed in the air in order to call forth the influence of that planet. This sign is by no means arbitrary, but rather is part of an intricate system.

In Hebrew, the word for the planet Jupiter is Sachiel, the roots for which are SKK (to protect or cover) and SChH (to trample).

This word itself has a numerical origin, and when this origin or base is distilled from the letters, it transposes into the following values:

S-60
A-1
Ch-8
H-5
(K-20)
I-10
L-30

(a) Intelligentiae Iovis

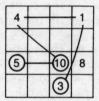

(b) Daemonis Iovis

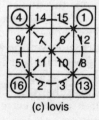

(c) Iovis

IX   Sigil formation

According to the Qabalistic tradition of *Aiq-bekr*,[41] or number transposition, the 0s may be dispensed with save for that of the number ten, leaving the numbers 6, 1, 8, 5, 10 and 3.

When we turn to the square, we see that the following pattern is obtained when tracing out some of these numbers (see diagram).

And when the numbers are combined through various simple permutations, as in, for instance, mere addition, we can see how the more complex sigil for Jove proper (Figure c) is generated, as below, by simply adding 8 and 5 for 13, 6 and 1 for 7, and so on in order to create the various sigils and harmonic patterns.[42]

In other words, the creation of the sigils – the ritual sign finally used in the rite – is precise indeed, expressing the various aspects of the celestial realm in the physical world in order to create certain effects. And the rationale for inscribing magic squares and other geometrical forms upon amulets is very much the same as that for sigils – to attract, or better, to manifest the appropriate higher, more eternal influences among the objects or events to be affected.

It is indeed through an understanding of the philosophy of magic that we can begin to see the profundity of Plato's apparently simple cosmological framework – for to say that the four elements are simply *qualities* of the One, are governed by geometric forms, and are in flux is but a cryptic expression of that which in magic reaches its full realization – that through communication with the governors, the celestial sources of the physical realm, one's actions and one's intent can reverberate throughout the intricate web of existence, sending ripples in every direction, much like a golden thread which one might weave throughout the warp and weft of a carpet.

The magician, in short, becomes a master of creation in a sense, a more conscious weaver in a pattern vaster than one can imagine. And yet he remains subject to the realm of cause and effect, himself also subject to the events and influences he brings into play. From this we can begin to glimpse not only the attraction of appearing to alter, even in the slightest way, the web of existence, but also its attendant responsibilities.

In any case the inscription above Plato's Academy in Athens still holds true: 'Let none who fail to understand geometry enter here.' Numbers, it is true, are hardly the key to the Mysteries. But without them, without the divine geometry, magic – door to mystery – will not be understood.

INVOCATION

In the modern world, deluged with the written word, it is difficult to recognize the original power which the alphabet has to recreate the world. Since, as we have seen, the purpose and meaning of magic is to recapitulate and recreate the world again within ourselves, to recognize our inherent unity with it, there can be no doubt that words form an intricate part of this aim, since they have the power to do that very thing. Reading, as Novalis said, is tantamount to entering another world.

And one can easily see that the word was created first, not only as a means of communication, but also as yet another means of realizing our place as microcosm. For what does the writer do, if not recreate the world anew upon the page? But whereas the writer creates images of the world – which is itself a reflection – [43] the magician traces existence back toward its Origin. The former use of words is the profane use to which Plato objected in the *Republic*; the magician, on the other hand, through invocation and sacred words, is uttering, manifesting that celestial realm and inasmuch as he does so is he realizing the Mind which underlies, and is, both realms.

Every magic tradition transmits the use of invocations, sacred words which serve as focus points and keynotes in the formation and realization of the celestial realm upon earth, opening new modes of perception. Music is closely related to – indeed, intertwined with – the use of invocation or sacred words because magic, like music, is the result of variations upon a theme and of harmonization. Since, as we have noted, our everyday world is made up of habit energy, then when that energy, like the notes of an instrument, is raised to a higher key, then a new harmony – a new perception – arises.

This is the function of the sacred word – the invocation and music used in ritual: to transmute the energy used in habitually recreating our mundane world each instant into a higher key. For our ego requires a constant flow of sapping energy to maintain itself, to continue the screens, barriers and habits through which we view and with which we react to the world around us. When the ego is transcended, that energy is transmuted into spiritual vitality, radiating 'magic.' The fact that ego is such a drain and barrier is visible in human senility, in which the person becomes a shell – a persona, a mask, almost a caricature of his or her former self – devoid of inner vitality. As ego is transmuted through discipline, invocation is used to activate those celestial aspects which were until then dormant within the magus. For in the intricate harmony of the cosmos, words – and letters – in invocation open channels 'to,' or set in motion resonances of Mind. For, in Pythagorean terms, in its essential form existence consists in harmonic vibration and the invocational word allows the magus to realize that harmonic vibration.

The first step toward the recognition of the power of invocation must be the realization that not only does every word contain worlds – but so does every letter. We already noted the relationship between vowels as the infilling spirit of a language and consonants as its external form, or meaning. But in addition each letter has a constellation of resonances and meanings surrounding it, imbuing it with power. The letter A, for example, is pivotal both in Sanskrit and in English, not only because it is the first letter of its language, sign of its inception and so of the creation of all things, but also because of its very tonality as the first expulsion of breath. It is the sound, in Sanskrit, of the Womb-syllable. A invokes the web of existence, reverberating through all things in their ebb and flux. In English the letter A also suggests the fall of one into two – the primal division into duality and the creation of all things – as well as the eventual resumption of two into one again within the individual. In Sanskrit, A is in polarity with Vaj, which is the diamond letter, symbol of light and clarity. And in fact the very sound of the Vaj – its resonance and vibration through partly closed lips – creates an angular, penetrating sound symbolic of knowledge. A is compassion, the womb. Vaj is knowledge, the light.[44]

It is interesting to note that Jacob Böehme, in his *Aurora*, changed *Mercurius* to *Marcurius* in order to denote and invoke the primal breath-syllable A, but, Böehme noted, disgruntled, someone changed it back, thinking he simply did not know how to spell properly.[45]

The power of letters is inherent in every language, although the antiquity of a given language invests it with that much more power, not least because such antiquity bestows the accumulated power and force of aeons of human use and concentration, but also because the more ancient a language, the closer it is to the original mantic purity of the seer in contact with language's divine source. This is the reason that Latin was used in most Renaissance magic invocations, and also because Latin was a more exclusionary language than mere English, French or German — but the derivative nature of Latin is also testimony to the gulf between Renaissance magi and the primordial tradition.

Language alone has the unique property of penetrating all the spheres of existence, of rending the veils, not only between us and our world, but between our world and other realms. In this lies the essence of the invocation of spirits. Again — to say that the spirits invoked are a manifestation of Mind is not to say that they are only a product of the individual human mind, for to do that would be to reduce them to mere psychologism and to deny the immense breadth and depth of the human microcosm. A spirit invoked has as much reality as ego and in some cases more, being of the celestial or mediate realms and maintaining therefore an existence independent, so to speak, of the ego. For this reason, any invocation must be undertaken with the utmost gravity, humility and purity — never the summary ordering-about of the popular misconception of magic. In magic one is dealing with realms greater than oneself and the danger, then, is not small.

It is for this reason that magicians guarded so carefully the sacred names and visualizations characteristic of the particular spirits with which they were familiar, for — even though the uninitiated would be unlikely to have any success whatever invoking them — if they were to do so there would be a good likelihood that they would encounter grave danger, not having the onepointedness to maintain equilibrium. Invocation is also closely associated with specific bodily centers, and if those centers are aroused without proper stability and depth, there is also a danger. Needless to say, however, this does not pose a great danger within a traditional culture, since the magus is there performing a transmitted function, for which he was born, and for which he is thus prepared and protected by virtue of his tradition.

There are, traditionally, three levels of spirits that can be invoked, levels that could be seen as rings of mandala.[46] On the innermost ring, closest to the magus, are those forms which he himself creates and visualizes. These are, more or less, the product of his own imagination. On the second level, farther out, are those spirits which are related to certain geographical areas – valleys, caves and mountains.[47] These earth spirits are sometimes connected with the traces of human thought and emotion in a certain area. And in any case it cannot be denied that certain areas have a very real presence, intangible, but altogether recognizable. This presence is due to a resonance between geographical features, or elements of the macrocosm, and their inner counterparts in man: they are the result of, a manifestation of, the hidden relation between man and the world around him. It is because of these hidden relations, manifested in the form of spirits in order to be comprehensible, that man is capable of harmonizing the weather and other natural phenomena, a capability found worldwide. Indeed, even if one is unable to consciously affect the weather, one still does so unconsciously, for as we have seen, each human being is a world in miniature and hence, when large numbers of anxious, confused and disoriented people congregate in a given area, natural phenomena are disrupted just by the effect of sheer numbers of people in that state of mind. It is for this reason that the true magus is necessary, for the magus must counterbalance the unconscious effect upon the world of those who know not what they do, with his own conscious and compassionate harmonization of those natural forces.[48]

The third level of the mandala is that of the devas – the angelic beings. These cannot be invoked in the same way the other two can, in that the devas are autonomous beings, tied neither to geographical locality nor to oneself, as a function and creation of the magus. For this reason the devas can only be petitioned and aspects of their influence received. In the traditional cosmology discussed earlier, the devas are those being in the celestial plane, of which this world is a reflection. In Plato's allegory of the cave, they are those who live outside the darkness of the cave, in the light.

Because this world – and we – are projections upon the screen of matter from that realm, however, the closer one draws to the celestial realm the clearer becomes one's 'double'

– in Egyptian *Ka*, and in Persian, Daēna.[49] That 'double' is 'created,' or 'resurrected,' insasmuch as the ego here is transcended, a transcendence which also implies a transcendence of the ordinary perception of space and time. Yet this 'double' is a reflection of Mind, of Sun, and is inherently no different from it. To a large extent the invocation of the angelic intelligences is the process of recognizing that 'double,' the 'soul,' through the intonation of those harmonic principles which correspond with different aspects of it, of Mind.[50]

The more an invocation penetrates and manifests in all three of those realms – earthbound, human and divine – the greater its force. But that force derives solely from the transcending of the ego and the realization of one's inherent unity with the Sun of existence, and therefore is concurrent with, and inseparable from, compassion.

That this is so is clear from the very nature of the invocation which, as spoken word, is pure vibration and energy, of which the phenomenal world is composed and which, when emitted, cannot help but have an incalculable effect, penetrating through temporary time and space. For as a manifestation of the Eternal – being ever the same – the invocation must necessarily be able to affect momentary temporal manifestations of being, which are like the bursting of a bubble, the flash of summer lightning. In fact, there is nothing surprising about this when one examines the matter closely – the life of a man passes by as nothing, as a wind through the trees, one moment here, the next moment gone, while the sound of an invocation passes on from century to century, ever the same, always awaiting the one who can bring it – and all its ramifications and meanings – to life again. In truth, the invocation has more validity, more existence, and more permanence than the one who invokes.

Yet at the same time the purpose of the invocation is to awaken those aspects of the eternal which dwell within each individual, to bring them 'back from the dead.' It is for this reason that the sacred syllables correspond to particular parts of the body, reminding one of its eternal aspects within temporality. The colors associated with the body are yellow, white, red, black and blue-green. In geometric form, they are square, circle, triangle, semicircle and triangle upon a semicircle. In Sanskrit seed-syllables, they are Ah, Va, Ra, Ha and Kha. Superimposed upon the body, these correspond to the legs and genital-urinary area, the lower abdomen, the chest, the throat and the head. In elemental terms, one finds these associated with Earth, Water, Fire, Air and Ether. Each of the spirits invoked corresponds to these colours and elements. One reason that the elements must be represented in invocational ritual is that they provide the material essence for the exteriorization of the spirits, for their visualization. In a sense, they lend corporality to them, providing a kind of ground. The highest spirit, being blue-green, is the transcendent Void, ether, the state of Emptiness, and can be given no form.

One other means for exteriorizing the spirits invoked, and giving them particular form (besides the use of elements), is that of the familiar, most closely associated with witchcraft. The familiar is an animal used to lend its vital energy to that which is invoked. Needless to say, the sacrifice of an animal is also associated with ritual for the same reason – it lends physical existence, vitality, to the spirit, and particularly to human creations and earth spirits. But the murder of an animal – of any sentient being – is an act of grave consequences, and carries with it great retributive force which will adhere to he who so disposes himself. Indeed, we can well say that these last two means of 'exteriorization' constitute infernal modes, tending as they do to reinforce the descending arc of the modern era into the subhuman realm, into destruction and chaos, and it is far from reassuring that they are increasingly seen in urban areas.[51]

It should be noted that invocation is not always spoken; the invocation may also take the form of the written word. In a sense, that is the function of the amulet, which is an inscribed object intended to draw down or manifest the various aspects of the celestial and supercelestial realms. The other means by which the written word may serve as invocation is as the twelfth-century Qabalist Abraham ben Samuel Abulafia taught: through the permutations of the Divine Names, in which he and his students would rise through the spheres into divine ecstasy by writing the Names faster and faster in the deep of the night until, wholly possessing and being possessed by them, the celestial realms were revealed.[52]

There is one aspect of invocation that must be reiterated: the difference between expulsion of the demonic and invocation of the daimonic. As noted briefly before, the invocation of devic, or celestial influences implies the expulsion of the lower, bestial or demonic creatures which ordinarily inhabit the mind of man – the demons of desire and hatred. For this reason the books of the magi throughout history have included rat-faced, cloven-hooved and terrifying demons which one must call forth – not because they are some external monster or pseudo-deity with which one must deal, but because these are the personifications of the forces within each of us which govern our everyday lives. Each time we manifest desire or aversion, we are bringing to life, signing a pact with, one of the demons of ego.

The reason the true magus – in the vernacular – 'consorts with demons' is to *expulse* those inner forms of ego. Every instant, every day that one lives without having expulsed those demons is a day lived in a tacit pact with them. In brief, we can say that 'magic' in the primordial culture is but the elimination of the demonic and irradiation of the daimonic or Divine through individual spiritual transmutation – a far cry from 'sorcery' – for the primordial magus is in fact expulsing the demons of desire and aversion, of ego and habit energy, in order that he may purify himself and thereby conduct natural forces in a compassionate, conscious way. There is no other way for the magus to act – and if he does turn to sorcery, as did the great Tibetan yogi Milarepa before his becoming the disciple of Marpa, he will reap immense karmic retribution and sorrow, as Milarepa himself testifies.[53] For these reasons, the popular image of the magician as one who 'consorts with demons' is at once ironic – with reference to a primordial era – and accurate, with reference to the emerging 'counter-tradition.'

Invocation, then, is essential to primordial ritual in that it is the means of penetrating and awakening those eternal centers within one which are the reflection and manifestation of all that is celestial, of all that is. Invocation, above all, must be enfolded within and part of a timeless tradition: one cannot invoke the Eternal with an unrooted, temporal invocation, for the very essence of an invocation is that it reaches into unfathomable aeons above and below, behind and ahead, being an irruption of the Eternal into the temporal, and not the other way round. For this reason no invocation can exist outside a transmitted tradition, the vessel in which the elixir is contained. That is why, for example, though we have the essential Gnostic Christian texts in the Nag Hammadi Library, with the inclusion of several of their invocations, including one with the specific names for awareness and recreation of the human body,[54] nonetheless that tradition died before 500 AD, and has not been resurrected: it has not been a living stream for fifteen centuries. Magic is the irradiating force of a religion; invocation is its timeless voice. And there can be no doubt that today, as ever, if one enters that living stream that voice can be heard once again, the voice that penetrates and permeates the web of existence, and all the realms.

LIVING STARS

Intoxication with the stars has always been an earmark of those deeply immersed in the spiritual journey. The modern North Africa Sūfi Shaikh Al' Alawi began, subsequent to his initiation by his Master, a series of writings upon the stars and planets, and his disciples relate that he would often spend the night in ecstasy, gazing at the stars.[55] It is significant that his first work was written about the stars – written, he said, because he could hardly contain his rapture, and the writing gave vent to it – because it underscores the intimate connection between the spiritual journey and the stars, a connection which is found to be reiterated in every theosophic book one encounters.[56]

Jacob Böehme, in his *Six Theosophic Points*, wrote that 'the elements are nothing but an image or a likeness, a moving existence of what is invisible and unmoving.' In addition, 'the stars likewise are an efflux of the qualities of the spiritual world, according to the separation of the separator, whose ground is the Word, or inseparable Will of God.'[57] Although some modern writers have sought to place Böehme and other Western mystics separate from Plato and Neoplatonism,[58] they are in fact indivisible, inasmuch as both echo the same universal truths. That this is so is evident even from the passage just quoted, for in it Böehme repeats, almost in the precise wording, a passage from the *Timaeus* in which Plato defines temporality and the elements as 'a moving likeness of Eternity.'

And it is here that the *mysterium magnum* of the stars begins to reveal itself: for the irresistible power of the stars lies, to begin with, in the fact that while apparently moving, they are eternal; changing, they are changeless. They are, as Böehme said, the efflux of the spiritual world. As the stars are invisible to the day and yet are its abstracted Ideal image, containing its Forms in the constellations, so is the spiritual world to the physical world, in that it too is invisible to the eye by day, and yet contains its eternal Forms and its celestial Origins.

This reciprocal polarity between the stellar and the terrestrial, and between the spiritual and the physical is a relationship more profound than can be elucidated in anything other than direct experience of it, but its ultimate resolution can be glimpsed in the central theme of this work: that all is Mind and the physical world is merely its reflection. As Böehme said:

> every life is a clear gleam and mirror and appears like the flash of a terrible aspect. But if this flash catches the light, it is transformed into gentleness and drops the terror, for then the terror unites itself to the light. And thus the light shines from the terrible flash; for the flash is the light's essence; it is its fire.[59]

Just as the stellar world is to the terrestrial, so the spiritual realm is to the physical: every life is born blind onto earth, and is frightened of the celestial, for the celestial appears to it as Void, as Nothingness. But as the life begins to catch the light, it begins to realize that the light is none other than its own essential nature, loses its terror of the Infinite celestial realms, and realizes its own divinity. It begins to embrace the celestial world of which this world is but a moving picture.

Yet the relationship between the stellar realm and the spiritual realm of essences is a mystery far deeper than a matter of simple analogy. For the stellar and planetary realms can never be seen merely as symbols, but rather must be seen as the sign of the ineradicable Pearl which is both within and without. The stars are not simply a symbol of that which is within: they are within. They are within Mind and are the manifestation of the Eternal being which is the soul. The stars are to the perishable cosmos and to the earth what the soul is, as the imperishable spiritual realm is to the body. And because the two – spiritual and physical – are not divisible, this is not only analogically true, but also, in a sense, 'empirical' description. The stars, then, are the perishable manifestation of the immortal soul and so are, while ultimately dissolved, still immortal by comparison to the transient earth, just as the soul – though dissoluble into spirit and then Mind – is still immortal by comparison to the fleeting house which is the body.

Thus it is that Plato in his *Timaeus*, when he discusses the nature of the soul's origin upon earth, begins with the Divine mixing of the souls in the *krater*, and continues to the division of the souls 'up into many souls, and the allotment to each soul of a star.' Mounted upon its star as upon a fiery chariot, the soul was then incarnated in the world of gain and loss, ruled by the laws of destiny and the six directions – before, behind, above, below, right and left. If the soul behaves evilly, it is dragged down by its accretions of ego, becoming animal – but if it behaves well, it returns to its native star where it lives in peace.[60]

The soul, then, in Platonic and Neoplatonic teaching is not only identified with, but united with a certain star. And it is for this reason that there is such a close tie between astronomy and the spiritual journey: inasmuch as there is no division between the microcosm and the macrocosm, so there can be no division between soul and star – and thus the study of the stars is the study of the inner world writ large upon the sky. For that reason, Edward Kelly entitled his work on alchemy *The Theatre of Terrestrial Astronomy*, for that is precisely what the spiritual transmutation through alchemy implies: the realization upon earth of one's celestial Origin – the realization of the star that 'is' one's soul and the constellations of the 'inner world.'

Hence magic practices, both Eastern and Western, depend not only upon the configurations and influences of the stars and planets on a given day – ritual astrology – but also upon the 'drawing down' of certain star-daemons. In the case of ritual astrology, and the determination of the most beneficent and malign hours for ritual, there are correspondence charts which one can consult, including those of Budge, from ancient Egypt, or Agrippa's. But the passive determination of what appear to be the relatively mechanical and impersonal workings and influences of the stars on given months, days and hours must be subsumed to the active invocation of particular star daemons, a practice common to both China and Europe. Yet it is quite naturally the former calculation that is better known, being deterministic, and therefore more accessible to those who cannot think in terms of the invocation and channeling of particular, invisible star daemons.

But the modern Taoist magician, Chuang-Ch'en Teng-yun, for instance, was quite capable of ignoring both requirements of auspicious hour and auspicious place, simply because by virtue of his powers of invocation, he was able to transcend merely deterministic influences and convert malignity into beneficence. The true magician is beyond the calculation of stellar and planetary influence, being able to invoke those he needs at will, but nonetheless, to be beyond such calculations he must have mastered them. Thus it is that magicians from East and West have taught that without knowledge of the proper auspicious hour and place, nothing can be accomplished, for as we have seen, primordial magic arose out of the divine harmony, sympathy and reciprocity of all things, a unity in which temporality must needs have its place.[61]

The difference between the calculation of celestial patterns and influences and the invocation of specific star-daemons can be seen as the difference between one who looks up from below at the patterns and weaving of the celestial realm, learning its map, its topography and its beneficent and malignant places, and one who, having fully mastered that topography, takes his place *in it*, able to traverse its paths and converse with its inhabitants. Without knowing its topography, one would have no way of knowing either its features or its inhabitants which, clearly, would be as foolhardy as to enter a wholly foreign country with no knowledge of its people, customs and landscape. The calculation of influences is a topic too well known, and too large to be delved into here: references for the stellar and planetary influences are widely available, and the presence of astrological columns in newspapers and magazines is testament to the ineradicability of the human recognition of celestial influences, though the value of such columns is less than nil, being utterly profane. While celestial influences are common knowledge – though their true calculation is not – the higher teaching of star daemons is virtually unknown, and hence it was that the earlier discussion of Neoplatonic and Platonic understanding of the connection between stars and souls was necessary in order to provide the schematic background for the teaching of the living stars, to which we now turn.

Since the Platonic and Neoplatonic understanding is in fact a gloss of magic and the teaching of the Mystery schools,[62] it comes as no surprise that the teachings suggested there – the numerical harmony of the cosmos, the ascent through the spheres, the stellar souls – in fact form a central part of magic. Pivotal among these is the teaching of the unity of star and soul. But to understand the full meaning of the stellar daemons, we must first look at the root of the word daemon, in order to eradicate the erroneous implications which have attached to the word over centuries of misunderstanding. The word daemon, or daimon, is derived from the Greek word *daiesthai*, which means 'to divide,' and is closely related to the ancient Germanic and Old English forms dī-ti, or tidīz, or tīd, all of which imply division into tide and time: emanation. Hence we find a direct relation to the Neoplatonic division of the world into spheres, or celestial emanations – or tides and waves. In the center is the timeless Light, and as one travels out, through the spheres, one encounters more and more time, and materia, and darkness as the Divine 'divides,' being reflected ever more lightly upon matter, until on the outermost or lowest circles, Divinity is hardly known at all. As dicussed earlier, this implies that the cosmos has Eternity at its center, surrounded by levels of being. Nearer Eternity are the stars whose lifespan is much longer than our own, which is at the lowest and most fleeting level, timebound. Human souls, then, are as stars in their longevity, but they too are finally subsumed to the Highest, to the blinding Light of the Eternal, of Mind. As Jacob Böehme said: 'the stars signify or denote the angels, for as the stars must remain unaltered to the end of time, so the angels must also in the eternal time of heaven remain unaltered.'[63]

The word daimon is the perfect denomination of soul, since it implies the apparent division of Mind in its reflection upon matter. Where its reflection is strongest – upon the stellar daemons – they are almost immortal, and exceeding bright. The reflection upon the planets is once removed from the stars, and more deeply immersed in time and space, while soul in man is yet once more removed. But only man is capable of realizing the nature of this reflection, being uniquely situated between matter and the Light of Mind.

Daimon, then, hardly designates some horned and malevolent being, as popular superstition would have it, but rather

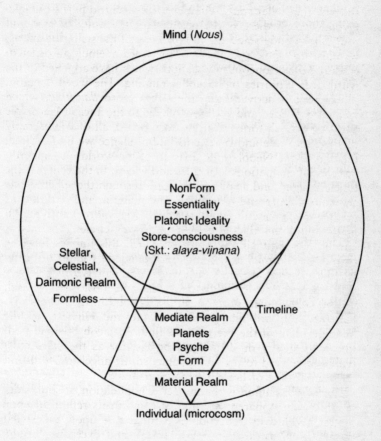

Mind (*Nous*)

∧
NonForm
Essentiality
Platonic Ideality
Store-consciousness
(Skt.: *alaya-vijnana*)

Stellar,
Celestial,
Daimonic Realm
Formless

Timeline

Mediate Realm
Planets
Psyche
Form

Material Realm

Individual (microcosm)

X   An Hermetic cosmological model

refers to those souls or beings which are closer to the Light at the center of the cosmos. What are called daimons in the West are *devas* in Buddhist cosmology, a word which derives from the same root – deus, divinity. Devas, too, are souls which are no longer as bound in time and matter, and so appear as stars, being more brilliant as they are closer to the Light of Mind. When the suffix is added to dai, making daimon, it also implies, in Greek, 'one who provides.' Hence the designation daimon implies a twofold meaning: in relation to Mind the daimon is divided, reflected in matter, but still is relatively pure energy and Light. In relation to man, however, the daimon is a provider, in that through daimons man can invoke and realize that Mind of which daimons, too, are but a reflection. The invocation of star daimons, then, is but a step on the path toward realization of Mind itself. It is for this reason that Plato said one whose life was free of defilement – as all magicians must be, this being a constantly reiterated requirement in magic texts[64] – will rise to his native star: that is, he will begin to realize his proximity to the Divine, eventually realizing that there is only the Divine, Mind.

Thus the central writings of one of the greatest Renaissance mages – Marsilio Ficino's *De vita triplici* – is oriented around its third section: *De vita coelitus comparanda*, which can be translated as 'On Guiding One's Life Celestially,' or, as D.P. Walker suggested, as 'On Instituting Life Celestially,' or, perhaps, 'On Attaining Celestial Life.' It is no accident that this section is the center of Ficino's philosophy of magic, for in it the relation of man to the stars, to the Divine, and to the material world around him is made clear: the cosmology of Neoplatonism and Hermeticism is both summarized and, at least in part, applied. *De vita coelitus comparanda* is largely concerned with the means by which the beneficent influences of the stars can be attracted, and the malevolent ones warded off or transmuted. The spectrum of means by which this is to be achieved is broad indeed: Ficino discusses the making of talismans (*images*), or amulets to be worn, the hearing and chanting of beneficent songs based upon cosmic Pythagorean harmonies,[65] the eating of the proper plants, the calculation of appropriate spots for dwellings or ceremonies, the scent of certain spices and incenses, the proper clothing and way of moving: in short, in Ficino, we see a resurgence of magic in a comprehensive, wholly unifying way as it had not been seen for many centuries. As noted earlier, magic is none other than the natural result of the process by which man realizes Mind and the celestial realm in earthly daily life, much as Zen Buddhism concentrates upon the need for realizing Buddhanature in the way one places one's shoes on the doorstep. Ficino's was not a quaint attempt to amuse himself with antiquary planetary charms, but rather an extraordinarily comprehensive and profound realization of the nature of magic and of traditional cosmology and understanding. The highest aim of both magic and religion must be to realize the celestial realm, to realize Mind in daily life, and it is this that Ficino outlines.

Ficino begins by delineating the traditional Neoplatonic cosmology, noting that the star daimons are cognizant beings with the ability to both act and to know that they act. But, having been freed from most of the constraints of the material, they are primarily radiant and so, says Ficino, they cannot be forced, only invoked. To this end, he went on, one should gain equilibrium by attracting primarily Solar, Jovial and Venusian influences. In order to attract Solar influences – most beneficial to the Saturnian philosopher – one would use all heliotropic gems and flowers, carbuncle, frankincense and myrrh, chryso-lite, honey, sweet calamus, saffron, cinnamon, the cock, swan, lion and beetle (scarab), and so on. Likewise, Jupiter may be attracted through steady and regulatory influences, including the lamb, the eagle and the bull, crystal, topaz and coral; Venus through things red and green, and so on.

The philosophical premises discussed in the section of this book dealing with natural correspondence reached perhaps its most comprehensive synthesis in Ficino. The purpose of natural correspondence is twofold: it is oriented toward achieving a mental equilibrium in the magician and, secondly, that equilibrium allows him to invoke or ascend toward his particular star daimon. Ficino himself says: 'as the quality and movement of any one of our particular members extends to things beyond itself, so the actions of the world's (the cosmic) principal members move everything, and the members of lower things easily receive from the higher ones *what they are prepared to offer*.'[66] The higher members, of course, are prepared to offer only that which the lower is capable of receiving – and they are capable of receiving only with the establishment of planetary equilibrium, the horizontal stabiliz-ation which allows and, at the same time, is a manifestation of the vertical ascent. To live among Solar, Jovial and Venusian influences implies that we are stabilizing the psyche and at the same time ascending toward Mind.

Only when the Platonic cosmological vision is grasped does the intent of the planetary and stellar correspondences in Ficino and Agrippa become clear. The star daimons so central to Ficino and Agrippa are in fact more real than any terrestrial phenomena, in that they are closer to and a more pure reflection of Mind. For this reason Ficino and Agrippa – and the Taoists – insist that one cannot will or force the daimons: they, in Reality, have more existence than we ourselves. Ego is an illusion. Hence when we invoke the stars, we are in fact invoking a purer aspect of that Mind of which we ourselves are a reflection.

It should not be surprising, therefore, that Taoist magic employs the invocation of star daimons in much the same way that Hermeticism does – as the recognition of Mind in a way that it can be apprehended, for it is in that very perception or glimpse of Mind that the magician's purpose is accomplished. By acting as a conduit for Mind, the magician channels the proper aspect of Reality, thus correcting the natural balance in a given area, be it through the expulsion of evil, the reconciliation of friends, or the accretion of blessings in a village.

The following is the spell for summoning the T'ien-chung star, along with its requisite Chinese symbols and talismans. As can be seen from the accompanying illustration, the talismans – and ritual movements – are in kind no different than those in Western magic manuscripts, though of course different tem-poral climates demand different application, just as music is modified in content, though not in form.

> Ch'ung-ch'ung, the sound of thunder!
> The nine heavens assemble together;
> From the trigram Ch'ien going forth,
> They enter from the trigram Chen.
> A sudden shower, followed by a rainbow,
> A single thunder clap!
> From the depths arises a rain dragon,

Evil forces' courage buried,
Demonic spirits' traces obliterated!
Thunder shakes a hundred Li!
A shattering fist, crushing, booming.
With your sound of thunder crashing,
Help me, send a fearsome wind,
Here and now I command thee, assemble,
Drumming, dancing hordes attend!
Chi-chi jü lü ling![67]

In Chinese Taoism, as in Western magic, the purpose of the magician is threefold. First, he himself rises to the level of the Eternal, of the Immortal. Second, he confers celestial benefits upon those about him, as well as upon those for whom he acts. Third, he bestows blessing upon and releases from torment those who are trapped in the material realm and wish to themselves rise toward the celestial.

The spells invoking the living stars, the daimons, are as much intended to awaken us as to invoke the daimons – but more than that, they are a testament of faith that we may one day, one instant, realize that which lies even beyond and in the stars: Mind. It is not an accident that the American Indians, like Macrobius and the other Neoplatonists, taught that the Milky Way is the great path that the soul travels to the celestial realm, its Home, with the cessation of the bonds of physical existence, and the soul's purification.

It is a description of 'empirical' Reality.

ALTAR AND ESSENCE

In order to perceive Reality both purification and sacrifice of the self are necessary, and it is this that the altar, which stands at the center of ritual, signifies. The altar implies purification because all that may come in contact with it are those things which have been cleansed of their base qualities and associations. The arthame and other elements of ritual may not have been – or are not used for other, profane purposes. And the altar implies sacrifice because just as the impure elements must be shed, stripped from the ritual implement, so must the comparable baseness and dross in the magus be laid aside.

71

XI   The symbol for *T'ien Chung*, a Taoist *daimon*

From the external point of view, this implies sacrifice. Before approaching the altar, one fasts and refrains from contact with impurity, from defiling oneself with mental confusion.

More than any other element of ritual, the altar signifies the recreation of the celestial world according to the magus's purified vision of it. One way of signifying this union of microcosm and macrocosm is through the use of 360 stones in its foundation. The 360 stones represent the union in the altar of both time – 360 days – and space – the 360 degrees of the horizon. This realization of the celestial realm of essences in the altar can only take place, though, through the 'turning about' at the source of habit energy – transcending the ego which perpetually recreates the world in our illusory image. Only when the 'self' is transcended can the deeper unity of man and the cosmos be manifested in the creation of an altar which is the sign of the sacrifice of self.

Without purification and sacrifice – without discipline – the approach to the altar is pointless, meaningless. The more this process of purification and sacrifice – of spiritual transmutation – is successful, the more habit energy is transmuted, the closer one approaches the recognition of the essential unity of oneself and the altar. For we ourselves are ultimately the altar upon which the magic takes place, in which the world is recapitulated and realized. Neither we nor the altar have a permanent and real existence: both are manifestations of Mind. And so, as Zen Master Dōgen said, to make an altar is to pile stupa upon stupa to make a stupa; it is to pile Buddha upon Buddha to make a Buddha.

It is in the altar, then, that we can see the essential inseparability, the meaning of 'orthodox' and 'magic' ritual. For like all phenomenal reality, the altar both exists and does not exist. From the phenomenal perspective, the altar exists as a manifestation of Form; yet from the perspective of Emptiness it exists not at all, nor do the artificial distinctions between 'orthodox' and 'magic.'

The levels of the altar imply the levels of consciousness or awareness upon which the ritual is manifested. In the creation of the altar, wood, stone, air, fire and water are used to invoke the various phases of phenomena: mineral, vegetable, animal, human and divine, or solid and liquid (frozen or heated) and gaseous. Each level is the same substance heated to create a higher form of existence, even though the original substance never changes. So too is the individual consciousness transmuted through the heat of ritual, paralleling the unfolding of creation which is mirrored in the creation of the altar.

In the altar we bring together the highest and lowest elements once again: the Divine is manifested upon, and in, stone. All of the intermediate elements – vegetable, animal and human – are manifested inasmuch as they are inseparable components of the human microcosm. When the ego is transmuted, these elements are brought forth, whereas in mundane life, they are obscured by habit energy. In magic – in the altar – all levels of being are manifested. This is why the magus places upon the altar representations of the animal, vegetable, and mineral realms, for by so doing he is manifesting the intermediate aspects of the microcosm.

Standing in the center of the spheres, of the magic circle, the altar is a stark reminder of our place upon earth as the uniter of the highest and lowest, of stone and the Divine. It stands as a reminder of the human journey and purpose – it signifies our entry into the temporal sphere, and points towards our ascent through the transmutation of the stone, the base earth around us, realizing the Divine by means of an unbroken transmission of the origional, primordial Path.

PART II

THE IRRADIATION
OF MAGIC

As we saw earlier, magic within the bounds of a traditional culture is but one discipline among many, part of an organic whole in which it acts to draw together, harmonize and stabilize, it acts on the mesocosmic level to maintain an equilibrium between the visible and the invisible, the physical and the celestial realms, not merely for the continuance of the culture, which would inevitably mean decay, but rather that the process of spiritual realization which is the Pole and meaning of every tradition might harmoniously take place. In other words, magic works upon a temporal, horizontal level to maintain harmony, in order that the vertical ascent might take place better. This horizontal stabilization can be seen in the great emphasis which the Renaissance Hermetics, for instance, put upon achieving planetary equilibrium through the balancing of Solar, Venusian, Lunar or Jovial aspects *within daily life*, using herbs, metals, clothing and gems.

This is the same purpose to be found in the arrangement of Plato's Atlantis, or Tommaso Campanella's *City of the Sun*: that is, these is the figure or type of the primordial culture, the culture of the Golden Age, represented most obviously by the concentric spheres of the two cities, and by their central temples each being of gold and silver. Plato observes that the gods then ruled by 'divine influence,' whereas Campanella has the priests of the Solar City using metals and herbs to ensure universal harmony, but the point is essentially the same: within a pure culture – that is, one dedicated to the Divine – all acts to further the spiritual ascent toward the Center (religion) and consequently that Center irradiates benevolent or harmonizing influences outward (magic), each reinforcing the other.

In these depictions of the primordial Tradition in its ideal form we can begin to realize the abyss, literal and figurative, which lies between us and the traditional world, and consequently between the modern view of magic and the original place it had in the human sphere. Indeed, the 'psychism' which today masquerades as magic is very nearly the farthest thing possible from its namesake in the traditional worlds.[1] For as we have seen, the history of magic and alchemy in the West is the chronicling of their progressive vulgarization and literalization, so that each became identified with the very basest of motivations. But nonetheless, within their remnants one can still glimpse their original purpose as, for instance, in the medieval accounts of witches who would strip themselves nude, anoint themselves with unguent and, flying out through the chimney of the house, would travel great distances to the bacchanalia of the Sabbat. Sometimes, it was said, an unfortunate witch would fall from the sky during such a journey, being hurt or killed. Virtually everyone is familiar with such tales – but few it seems are aware of their origin in tradition, in esoteric analogy.

For every aspect of the tales of witches related above is a vulgarization of esoteric analogy, of contemplative revelation. The stripping of clothing is an analogy found most commonly in the Gnostic Christian writings, although it recurs in Neoplatonism and in the Hermetic tradition, and refers to an intermediate level of consciousness in which the body – the fleshly garment – appears to drop away, perhaps related to the condition in Zen Buddhism in which 'mountains are no longer mountains.' In terms of the Qabalistic Tree this can be said to correspond to the ascent from the world of Malkuth, of temporal 'clothing' above the realm of psyche into the celestial sphere. The anointing of the witches refers to the transmutation of the human body into its higher celestial 'form' – and the sign of that change is shining, luminescence, of which unguent is an analogous symbol. This body becomes 'transparent' inasmuch as 'the other' is made real, and the culmination is the merger of the two – celestial and physical – into one. The unguent is then the symbol of the anointing of the spirit.

And the final element of the witches' preparation – leaving the house through the chimney – is also a literalized analogy. For by 'the house' we should read 'merely physical, temporal existence.' The chimney is in fact a symbol of the realms of the human body termed *chakras* in Hindu teaching; at the base of the chimney we find the fire, or *kundalini*, the basal energy of existence and transformation. The fire is the intense heat of alchemical concentration and discipline by means of which one, like smoke, rises through the 'tunnel' which stretches up behind the navel, through the heart, the throat, the crown of the head, and up into Boundlessness.[2] This 'tunnel' also remained a prominent analogy in Sūfism and in Persian descendants of Gnosticism.

But the most telling aspect of the tales of the witches is their alleged incidence of 'falls from the sky.' For taken in its original, analogical context this can only be due to their 'lack of control,' to the virtual impossibility of spiritual ascent and realization in a tradition divided, in which magic and orthodoxy are artificially opposed and so falsified, debased. The falling of the witches echoes the falling away of the West from its Origin; truly a fall from grace in every sense of the word.

And this fall does, in general, correspond to a historical continuum, at the inception of which we can see the Golden Age, the primordial tradition of which Atlantis and the City of the Sun are representations, and at the end of which we can see the Age of Iron, of which even Zamyatin's *We* is insufficient representation, though perhaps it draws close. Consequently we can say with some justification that in the West this continuum can be seen as the progressive 'erasure' of the three-world cosmology, beginning with the expulsion of Origen and the exclusion of *Nous* from 'orthodox' theology, gaining strength with the denial of the celestial realms which marked the Renaissance, and culminating in the present era with the disequilibrium or 'fall' of the psyche.

It is necessary then, before we examine further the manifestation or irradiation which we term magic within the primordial tradition, to first look closer at the opposite of the spectrum: that of 'psychism.'

THE IRRADIATION OF MAGIC

IN THE REALM OF PSYCHE

According to Islamic tradition,[3] the rebellion against the Divine takes place not in the realm of the body but in the realm of the psyche, and upon reflection we can see why this is so, for it is only in this mediate realm, aspects of which are symbolized by the seven planets, that such a thing *could* take place, the higher celestial realm 'partaking' more directly of the Divine and so being self-sufficient,[4] as it were, immune to delusion. This 'rebellion' of the soul corresponds, in Platonic thought, to the disorder wrought in the psyche when entering the sublunary realm of the senses, for here an originally 'positive' influence may become 'negative,' distorted.[5] In brief, each of the planets was, when in proper harmony and equilibrium, a *positive* aspect of the human individuality – but when they were out of order, or unbalanced, they then came to represent their own inversion, so to speak, due to the turbulent confusion effected in the soul by the 'gusts' of the senses.

In its proper place, and in harmony, Saturn is Intellect and closest to the celestial realm – but its inversion is mere reason, which seeks to usurp the functions of the transcendent, to mimic the gods, and so introduces disharmony amongst all the other planets, for instance. Only in the realm of the psyche, or perhaps better, the soul,[6] does this dual quality obtain, and so it is only here that the rebellion against the Divine, the attempt to usurp the place of the King, can take place.

Hence we can see why so much emphasis was placed, particularly in Renaissance magic, upon the harmonization of planetary influences within the individual – for if this realm is in disarray, then no ascent to the celestial realm is possible, nor indeed one's proper functioning within the culture. Disarray in this realm means that all one's relationships – to nature, to other people and, perhaps most, to Divine or celestial influence – are skewed, confused.

But the Renaissance itself consisted in nothing if not the exclusion or rejection from the Western mind of the celestial or angelic realms[7] consequent upon the 'triumph' of rationalist Aristotelian thought, and so since that time we have been dwelling ever more in the realm of *mundus medius*, of psyche. With this in mind, the nature of the modern attraction to psychic phenomena, and to bizarre forms of 'spirituality' under

78

many guises becomes clear: having cut himself off from his traditions, but realizing the barren nature of a purely materialistic point of view, man seeks to *recreate for himself* that which he has lost. This attempt at recreation, though, is necessarily confined to the psychic realm, 'below' the realm of the planets and so represents a triumph of the irrational under the guise of spirituality.

We can see this tendency, which can best be termed 'psychism,' most clearly in the various attempts at 'visualization' techniques, common to psychologists and 'magicians' alike, as to the 'neoshamanic' and to those who wish to welcome in a 'new age': all seek to 'guide' one, through a kind of inversion of spiritual disciplines, into 'higher states.' But these states, being outside tradition and confined to the realm of psyche, can only lead to solipsism[8] and dissolution, being in fact a human attempt to usurp the place of the Divine, and so being, in the strictest sense of the word, satanic. This tendency also appears in the advent of artificial intelligence and the computer, both of which demand one's attention to the exclusion of the natural world.

In other words, in the world of primordial spirituality the individual, the mesocosm of culture, and the cosmos itself mirror one another, so that the planetary aspects of the individual are not distorted by attachment to the lowest, material sphere but rather reflect their higher, original counterparts, so that each level of these concentric spheres acts in harmony with all the others just as planets revolve around a Sun. But in the modern era, at the opposite end of the continuum, the individual is 'aiming' in a direction precisely antithetical to the former – that is, down into the sea of chaotic matter and away from the Sun, seeking to create the world after his own image, thereby creating a 'civilization' ever more artificial, disharmonious, and necessarily headed for absolute dissolution, being based as it is wholly upon the pursuit of illusion.

The attraction to psychism and to the creation of artificial intelligence lies in precisely this: both are human attempts to create absolutely artificial, sham worlds after one's own image, having virtually exhausted the possibilities of manipulating and transforming the material world itself, and indeed, it seems certain that as the negative consequences of technical manipulation and exhaustion of the physical world become more apparent – along with widespread economic disjunction, and a growing sense of the futility of 'ordinary life' – there must needs be a growing attraction toward retreat into absolute artifice and illusion, represented on the one hand by psychic visions and 'astral travel,' and on the other by the images of the computer.[9]

But at precisely the nadir, when the absolute antithesis of the traditional realm in all its aspects is reached – that is, when the 'magic' of modern man culminates in total illusion, absolutely divorced from Reality – then it must vanish, being after all but an illusion, and the Golden Age of another world and another cycle will begin, causally united to our own.

It is with this era in mind – the origin of tradition past and future – that we turn to examine the nature of magic and its irradiative effects within the world of primordial spirituality.

TALISMANS, TIME AND SPACE

There can be little doubt that the best way of approaching the irradiative nature of magic within the primordial culture is through an understanding of the nature of talismans, the creation of which lies at the very heart of the discipline. But to understand the nature of the talisman we must first recognize the original meaning of the word, which entered Europe as the Arabic word *tilsam*, which derived from the Greek words *telein*, meaning to fulfill, complete or consecrate, and *telos*, meaning completion, fulfillment or ultimate state. For in the etymology of the word we can begin to glimpse the original meaning of amulets or talismans.

As we have seen, man occupies in traditional cosmology a unique place, situated as he is between the higher and lower realms, and because of this uniqueness he is able to ascend toward the Divine by means of religion – and simultaneous with this ascent is he able then to 'radiate,' to act as intermediary for Divine and celestial influences. Thus in the Hermetic cosmology man is able, by virtue of this ascent, to also raise up or animate the world around him: in short, by himself attaining the Divine state insofar as it is possible for him, man is also then able to *consecrate (telein)*, to bring to fulfillment and completion the Divine and celestial nature within the natural world as well. In this lies the real meaning of the talisman, which is but the 'bringing out' or realization of the Divine or celestial nature within a given object, be it stone or wood, by virtue of the unique place of the human being as mediatrix. Henceforth that object itself acts in a mysterious way to further harmonize and 'draw up' that which surrounds it, just as within the primordial culture as a whole the magus is one who acts to irradiate benevolent or equalizing influence about him.

In Islamic culture this irradiative effect is recognized by the word 'barakah,' which refers to the benevolent influence of a sage or saint, while in Japan the words 'joriki' and 'tariki' convey to some extent a similar meaning: that is, the irradiation of spiritual power in order to further the spiritual realization and liberation of all beings.

But a talisman, like all aspects of magic, is a physical manifestation of eternal principles, principles which do not vary from place to place, although the specific representation of them might. It is in fact at once a drawing forth from and a channeling towards earth of celestial influences by virtue of the magus. Yet without the proper 'channeling,' and the tradition from which that which is 'channeled' wells, a talisman is at best nothing more than a scrap, a bit of stone invested with superstition.

Nonetheless, there can be no question that talismans may be made, since they have existed in every culture and every time from aeons immemorial, from the ancient Egyptians to the third-century Gnostics, from the fifteenth-century Renaissance magicians to China, from the Eskimo to the Maya. The reason modern man has difficulty accepting amulets and talismans – perhaps more than other kinds of magic – is that they imply that the flat, two-dimensional way in which we tend to view matter, despite the discoveries of physicists, may be myopic in the extreme. Amulets imply that matter – which we tend to assume is inanimate – may in fact be animated, and partake of a kind of third dimension of intangible but very real influence, influence which is wholly related to the unity of all things in Mind, and which cannot be measured or quantified in a two-dimensional way. The fact that stone can be invested with specific influences which it then radiates should hardly surprise us, but it nonetheless does.

The amulet or talisman is, like the ritual itself, a unifying of the polarities, uniting time and space in one instant of being, manifested in the influx of the celestial or Zodiacal influences in the stone. It is for this reason that many amulets are constructed as directional compasses within which are the planetary signs, the angelic names, and the Highest Names. The amulet varies, of course, according to that which it is intended to invoke, hold and radiate. A magus might create a malign amulet if it were necessary to draw such influences from himself, to purify himself. However, because of the very nature of its symbolism, as a manifestation of the highest in the lowest, most talismans must of necessity be beneficent.

For this to be so, the magus must take care that the talisman be constructed according to the proper metal, and at the proper time of day, which can be calculated by the lists below. Most of all, though, the magus must take care that the planets invoked by the amulet be in their beneficent phases at the time of the amulet's construction, or the talisman will manifest its opposite, negative influence. The stones associated with the planets are as follows:

The Sun: gold-coloured (hyacinth, topaz, chrysolite)
The Moon: white stones (diamond, pearl, crystal, opan and beryl)
Mars: red stones (ruby, haematite, jasper, bloodstone)
Mercury: neutral stones (agate, carmelian chalcedony, sardonyx)
Jupiter: blue stones (amethyst, turquoise, sapphire, jasper, blue-diamond)
Venus: green stones (emerald, sapphire)
Saturn: black stones (jet, onyx, obsidian, black coral)

The metals associated with the planets are, Gold with the Sun, Silver with the Moon, Iron with Mars, Mercury with Mercury, Tin with Jupiter, Copper with Venus, and Lead with Saturn.[10]

In general, the aim of the amulet creator is to recapitulate the three realms of the cosmos within the stone or metal. In the center is the Divine Name, surrounded by the signs of the planets and constellations, or the Zodiac, and then, finally, the four directions of the physical world. In those amulets designed to draw in specific planetary aspects, however, the entire amulet may be devoted wholly to that planet, including its specific metal, magic square, sign and intelligence.

The justification of the making of amulets in the West, during the Renaissance, derived in large part from a pivotal passage in the *Asclepius* of Hermes Trismegistus, the only reference in the *Corpus Hermeticum* to actual magic and, significantly, a reference to the investing of celestial power into physical objects. The passage, in part, is as follows:

> Of all the marvels this most deserves admiration: that man
> has been able to discover the divine nature and, indeed, to
> produce it. Since our ancestors erred greatly about the
> doctrine of the gods, being unbelievers[11] and not turning
> their minds to worship and the divine religion, they
> discovered an art by which they made gods. To this art, once
> discovered, they added an appropriate strength drawn from
> universal nature, mixing it well in. Because they could not
> create souls, they evoked the souls of daemons or angels and
> introduced them into the holy images and the divine
> mysteries; and from these the idols acquired the power of
> acting beneficently or malignantly.[12]

As can be seen from this passage – and from the earlier discussion of the nature of the stars and planets – when an amulet is constructed, it is imbued not merely with the influence of certain planets, but rather is designed to invoke those eternal principles or daemons of which the planets and stars are the outward, physical sign. It is in order to underscore this understanding that Macrobius, in his *Commentary On the Dream of Scipio*, said that 'we must remember that the names Saturn, Jupiter and Mars have nothing to do with the nature of these planets but are fictions of the human mind which "numbers the stars and calls them by name." '[13] That is, that which we perceive as the planets are only their shadow, or image, and the purpose of the amulet is to recapitulate their celestial Form, or daemon.

The investing of influences – the animation – of a stone is related to the process of alchemy, in that both imply the process of manifesting the Sun of the highest realm in the lowest element of the physical world: stone. Both involve the transmutation of stone into something which is both stone and intangible spirit, and are therefore intimately tied to the greatest mysteries of both alchemy and magic, the mysteries surrounding the purification and realization of the soul and of heaven on earth and, indeed, in earth.

The value of amulets is much like that of the actual transmutation accomplished in alchemy – that is, they are the sign and seal of the work, being the transmutation of the *prima materia* into something exquisite. The transformation of lead into gold is a sign of the culmination of a very extended process of spiritual transformation, and is by no means the central aim of alchemy any more than the creation of talismans, as such, is the aim of magic. Both are simply byproducts of an involved inner process and struggle. But in both magic and alchemy the metaphoric and spiritual imagery was taken only literally, so that the intricate process of spiritual transformation was subsumed to the possible byproducts of that process, the forms of magic. In the case of magic this resulted only in the attempts to create amulets, or follow the directions for a given ritual with no knowledge of inner meaning, hence rendering them utterly useless, seemingly without validity. When enough such ignorant attempts were made, the vision of magic and alchemy fell into disrepute. But the decline of alchemy, which ran along much the same lines – due to the rise of the 'puffers' who took directions literally and scurried to their laboratories and to financial ruin – does not invalidate the existence of a true and higher alchemy.

Contrary to popular belief, neither the creation of talismans in magic nor the creation of gold in alchemy lie at the center of magic and alchemy. Rather, animation of matter in both cases marks the transmutation of the magus himself. As to the actual transmutation of matter: the true magus is guided by knowledge and compassion, so that if the creation of an amulet furthered the realization of Mind then, naturally, he would employ it as an extension of beneficent influence. For the value and meaning of talismans – of any magical practice – lies in the extent to which it furthers the awakening of Mind in every sentient being.

The irradiating effected by talismans signifies, on another scale, the harmonization of the culture and the macrocosm by virtue of a turning toward the Divine, much as a heliotropic plant turns toward the sun. And so it suggests the nature of a similar relationship between primordial man and the natural world: the relation of man and weather.

ACCLIMATION AND TRANQUILLITY

In the anthropological view of magic, magic arose solely to help primitive man cope with a hostile world, and as soon as he developed the skill to conquer the natural world, he immediately shed primitive magic as a snake sheds a skin it has outgrown. However, as we have seen, this view is anything but accurate, magic being far more inherent within humanity than rationalists are willing to admit. For in fact magic is but a manifestation of very specific human aspirations – indeed, of the highest human aspiration: liberation from the realm of birth and death, knowledge of who we are. This meaning cannot be obtained by rational attempts to ferret it out; rather, it is a result of great discipline and immense inner struggle, of a 'turning about in the deepest seat of consciousness.' In the primordial culture magic arises from and draws toward this end – it is but a byproduct of that path.

Nonetheless, the erroneous anthropological view of magic – as the misguided attempts of primitive man to deal with a 'hostile' environment – is based upon one valid argument, for surely one of the most important practical elements of the harmonization we call magic, for one who lives upon the land, is the harmonization of the weather. If it hails, if there is drought, modern man is at present inconvenienced, but one living on the land may well die. For this reason – because his relation to nature is immediate – harmonization with the weather was a necessity for primordial man. But it is hardly the 'reason' that magic came to exist – for magic is, as we have seen, but a natural facet of the true relationship between man and the cosmos.

Man as a microcosm is engaged in an intimate dance – a unity within flux – with the macrocosm and all its ebbing, surging currents. Foremost among these currents – since it is most tangible – is the weather. Jung once said that there was a closer relationship between humanity and the weather than anyone now suspected, and that the collective disposition of a city or an area directly affected the weather experienced there. And it does seem self-evident that there is a direct connection between the collective anxiety and paraonia of the modern city and the very high modern incidence of earthquakes, deluges, and other destructive weather phenomena.

In fact, there can be no doubt that human beings influence, as they are influenced by, the weather. As to the latter, sensitivity to impending storms is often found among arthritic or rheumatic people and nearly everyone has felt the delicate shifts of mood that accompany a change in the weather from sunny and warm to cold and grey. All this is well accepted – yet when the equation is reversed, and one speaks of people affecting the weather, scoffers abound. Nonetheless, as the Hermetic treatise entitled *Tabula Smaragdina* has it: 'as above, so below.' That is, the relation of the microcosm and macrocosm, as well as the relation of the earthly and the celestial realm, are very much reciprocal, mirror images. If the weather affects people, then people affect the weather. And, indeed, the evidence for directing the weather is far too universal for it to be spurious.

From the Indian shaman to the European witch, from the African witch doctor to the Tibetan magician, one of the most feared magical abilities is that of directing the weather. When Alexandra David-Neel entered Tibet, she said she felt malevolent forces congregating about her, and more than once her way was blocked by extremely rough weather which her guides immediately attributed to the local magicians barring her way. In medieval Europe it was said that witches could direct a hailstorm upon a neighbour's crop; in fact trials of cases of this abound. In Taoist China similar incidents are taken for granted, as they are in Tibet: one's first recourse is to another magician to counter the weather direction. In Europe the witch was denounced and burned; in China the wronged party simply went to a stronger magician who reversed the spell and defeated the weaker magician, plaguing him with the very spell he had cast.

One must note, however, that the 'modern' magus does not so much create hailstorms or other such phenomena as direct them – as Wayne Shumacher observed.[14] The reason for this is clear inasmuch as it exemplifies the historical continuum discussed earlier: that is, the more 'distanced' the magus from the primordial tradition, the more he is forced to rely upon effort of will and attempts to control or direct the elementals – as 'Abramelin the Mage' said is necessary – rather than upon the beneficent influences of the celestials and upon the harmony and equilibrium wrought by virtue of spiritual transmutation.

In planetary terms, 'malign' weather would be associated with the most 'malign' planets: Saturn, Mars and perhaps the Moon, which of course is traditionally associated with water, rain and fertility. On the other hand, Jupiter, Venus and the Sun tend to be 'beneficent,' though the application of their influence is dependent upon the establishment of the proper equilibrium, particularly the Solar and Lunar equilibrium.

But despite the prevalence of the direction of 'malign' weather in the popular conception of magic, it is needless to say the inverted image of weather magic, for clearly the pacification of the weather for the common good is much more aligned with the aim of the primordial magician: universal compassion, which is a natural aspect of the spiritual transmutation. Pacification not only benefits the populace, but the magus as well, inasmuch as pacification of disruptive weather corresponds to the pacification of the passions. This pacification of the weather is accomplished in a similar manner worldwide: the magus acts as a conduit for and an intensifier of natural local magnetic currents. In China the science of natural living currents in the topography is known as *feng shui*. There it is taught that the dragons fly over the land in the spring, carrying with them the beneficent currents of spring – growth, green and warmth – which follow the natural flow of the land, flying on specific, well-charted dragon lines. The magus simply aids the dragon's flight. In an ancient Chinese text it is said that as fish cannot see water and man cannot see air, so dragons cannot see the earth in which they exist. In a sense, it is the purpose of the magus to be the eyes for all.

Similar lines of natural currents are to be found in Australia, where after a certain number of years, the magi follow the lines on foot to renew their vitality and to aid their flow, stopping at particularly significant sites. Both the science of *feng shui* and the aboriginal practice suggest a responsibility to the weather and to the land – a specifically human responsibility – now neglected. In fact, though there is much talk of 'ecological awareness' at present, in general it takes the form of manipulative techniques and quantitative measurements which deny or ignore the exquisite unity between man and the cosmos upon which magic is based. And so attempts to *direct* the weather rather than to harmonize it are in fact much closer to the manipulative attitude of the modern era, and perhaps are allied with it in motive. In brief, the remark of Arthur Herzog that science more and more becomes magic takes on a new, not to mention sinister, implication.

In any case if, as we have suggested, the turmoil of the modern mind is responsible at least in part for the modern increase in foul weather, earthquakes and volcanoes, then conversely, a tranquil mind will have a calming effect upon the same phenomena. And, worldwide, this is held to be the case. John Blofeld told of a village in China that had been under a drought for a very long time – long enough so that cattle and other animals were dying – and the people were endangered. After a time, the villagers called for the aid of an aged Taoist sage, who came to the village and secreted himself in one of the huts for three days, at the end of which it rained. The villagers imagined all manner of strange rites, and finally one of them was bold enough to ask what he had done to accomplish the bringing of rain.

'Ah,' said the sage, 'when I arrived the Tao was out of balance. I stayed three days until it rained, until the Tao was balanced.'

Likewise, there is a story of Zen Buddhist who was travelling when he came upon a distraught woman – her husband had been out all night carousing and drinking, and was a man easily angered. She didn't know what to do. The monk sat down in the house, and began to do zazen, sitting through the night beside the drunken husband, who had stumbled in. By the time the monk had finished his zazen, the husband had given up his drunkenness, and his anger soon abated as well. This capacity to take upon oneself the turmoil around one is echoed in Sūfism: al Ghazālī, in his treatise *On the Duties of Brotherhood*, told of a Sūfi whose brother Muslim had become argumentative and had begun to neglect the way. He began to fast and fasted for forty days, until so weakened he drew near death. But as the time of death drew near, his brother, realizing the blindness of his actions, renounced them and returned to life. Then, too, there is the story of the Sixth Patriarch of Zen Buddhism, who went into a whorehouse and spent the night in zazen. Before he left, one of the prostitutes approached him and asked whether she should be reproached for her life. In reply, he wrote the following poem:

> The Buddha sells the doctrine,
> The patriarchs sell the Buddha,

The priests sell the patriarchs,
She sells her body
That the passions of all beings may be quieted.
Form is Emptiness; the passions are Bodhi.

All of these incidents bear in common the assumption of an inherent linkage between the inner and the outer: the tranquillity of one mind calms not only the minds of others, but the weather, the natural phenomena, as well. In terms of Buddhist philosophy, this could be expressed as follows: existence can be conceived of as a stream; one who enters the Way of Buddhism is referred to as 'one who has entered the stream.' In this conception, the individual ego is seen as a whirlpool or vacuum which draws in debris and flotsam. The speed with which it draws in debris – its force – is determined by the strength of the ego's passions or revolutions. When this force is transcended, or 'turned about,' then the stream flows freely, without inhibition, confusion or turmoil. Similarly, when the Scylla and Charybdis of the individual ego is quelled, both human and cosmic relationships are necessarily smoothed, since all are one with that stream. It is this relationship – symbolized by the whirlpool in the stream and its dissolution – that lies at the heart of the harmonizing of weather, of the natural world.

This unity can be seen, too, in the ancient Dionysian and Bacchic rites. For both rites were celebrated in the spring – like the Australian and Chinese renewal of the earth currents – in order that the natural world function more smoothly, freely. Just as the Chinese magicians would empty their mind of passions and extraneous thoughts through fasting and meditation, so the Bacchic and Dionysian celebrants would empty themselves through the ecstatic rites of spring, dancing to frenetic music and abandoning their ordinary habit energy in order that the natural energy rising in the spring be channeled through them into their land. The Bacchic and Dionysian agricultural rites were intended to function, on a broad scale, in the same way that the Zen Buddhist monk's zazen in the house of an angry drunkard effected a change: by the effusion of tranquillity amid storm and turmoil, harmonizing and restoring equilibrium.

On an even larger scale, the equilibrium produced by harmonizing an entire city is the basis of the many Renaissance utopias, from the New Atlantis of Bacon to Tommaso Campanella's *City of the Sun*. Campanella's *City of the Sun*, for instance, was governed by the center palace in which the priests, who were in absolute union with their world, lived. In the center of the elaborate palace were images and amulets, each designed to harmonize with planetary influences and unify the kingdom, not only pacifying the passions of the people, but maintaining beneficent weather and other natural phenomena as well. This grandiose vision, however, is dependent upon the orientation of the individuals in the polity toward realization of their inherent nature, much as planets orbit a Sun. In the fragmented modern world, however, this vision seems distant indeed – yet was it not also distant when Bacon and Companella – and indeed, when Plato himself put it forward in the *Republic*? The utopian city is read first on the level of the individual, and then at that of the community.

The equilibrium of a state, like the equilibrium of the weather and other natural phenomena, depends upon the equilibrium achieved by the inhabitants in that area. The utopia without cannot exist without the utopia within. But inasmuch as each individual's capacity for understanding differs, it is necessary that some assume more of the responsibility for that equilibrium, much like the philosopher-king in Plato's *Republic*. Shelley was wrong, for it is not the poet who is the unacknowledged legislator of the world – it is the magician. The poet is but a subdivision of the magi, creating with words the facsimile of what for the magician is reality itself. The poet sings of the celestial world – the magus lives there. And for that reason, his responsibilities are the greater.

The apocryphal Taoist and Zen Buddhist incidents, the harmony of man and the cosmos, the very nature of magic itself suggest that the place of the magus in society is the antithesis of that attributed him in popular superstition. Far from being the scourge of society, bent upon its destruction and his own greed, the magus, by virtue of the way in which magic works – by emptying oneself – must be the epitome of compassion and humility.[15] For magic, as we have seen, is based wholly upon the transcendence of the ego, and of habit energy, in order to channel divine forces and powers. In a very real sense, the magus must sacrifice himself for others, 'giving up' the ego in order to benefit those around him. Nowhere is this seen more clearly than in weather harmonization, for by denying himself, by breaking down that illusory whirlpool in the stream, the magus – a bodhisattva – benefits every sentient being, allowing the rain to fall when it should and the sun to shine when it must – absolute, untainted spontaneity. As a Zen Master once said, 'When I sit, I just sit!' So, too, when it rains, it just rains. But to achieve such a level requires intense effort and discipline – if not, we would all be magicians. Inherently, we are. The difficulty lies in realizing it.

PRIMORDIALITY AND THE SUPERNATURAL

Strictly speaking, it is impossible to refer to 'supernatural' phenomena within the context of a culture that retains its primordial nature, since within such a culture there can be no artificial opposition of 'natural' and 'supernatural' – this dualism is a product of the modern rationalist point of view. Rather, within a tradition that retains any degree of primordiality, phenomena which we term supernatural are to that same degree considered natural – that is, a result of given causes and consequent effects, or in other words, of principles. It is because modern man has cut himself off from his origin, because he is no longer aware of the traditional Hermetic cosmology and philosophy, that he posits an erroneous heading – the 'supernatural' – to dismiss that which is for him at best void, or else a swirling mass of 'superstition' (literally: that which is 'held over').

Virtually everything which today is labeled superstition or supernatural is in reality but the residue of the primordial culture – which is inherent in man, do what he will to ignore it – and so is quite explicable in terms of the traditional cosmology. However, needless to say, we cannot here do more than offer a few instances of 'extraordinary phenomena' which take on a new light when returned to their proper place, becoming part of a more coherent whole. One of the most important of these – since it occupied such a central place in diverse cultures – is that of the prophecy, or oracle.

Two of the cultures in which the oracle played an important role were those of Greece and Tibet: in Greece the function was served most notably by the priestesses at the famed Temple at

Delphi whom even Socrates consulted during his search for a wise man, and there were other such Temples as well; in Tibet the same tradition was preserved even into the present century, and up until the lamentable forced exodus from that country in recent years nearly every important monastery also had an Oracle, continuing a tradition which stretched far back before the advent of Buddhism or even Bön-po, to the very dawn of humanity. The oldest of these Oracles in Tibet was that established at Samyé by Padmasambhava, but the central or State Oracle was at Nächung, to which all others were subsumed. Tibet was in fact the last culture on earth to retain in so pure a form its primordial tradition, and so we are fortunate to have at least the compelling accounts of two instances of Oracular possession by Lama Govinda in his *The Way of the White Cloud*.[16] There the Oracle is described as it must have taken place through all history: an individual who, by virtue of his function, is willing to become wholly dispossessed of his body through trance and to allow the divine powers inherent within a tradition to take over, using his being to convey that which is infinitely beyond the human realm. One can see the danger inherent in such a dispossession of the habit energy of the ego, the possibility of insanity or worse, but from this the Oracle is protected by virtue of the impeccably preserved tradition, the power of which excludes the malignant forces.[17] The purpose of the Oracle, then, was once again that of harmonization with the Divine, for through the self-sacrifice of the priest, an answer was given from an inconceivable power in order that the culture might continue its sacred function.

For this reason the prophetic utterance is encoded in paradox: the paradox or cryptic saying contains within itself the polarities, signifying their resolution in the higher realm, and when that understanding is brought down to the phenomenal, as in prophecy, it contains within its expression more than can either be said or understood in ordinary language. Thus, as Macrobius and Porphyry said, the prophetic utterances of the ancient Greek sibyls were intended not as mere answers or conclusions, but rather were seeds from which the answer might grow if sought further. This must necessarily be so, since the true resolution of any temporal problem can only be found in the realm of unity. Hence a prophetic utterance, like the *koan* in Zen Buddhism, in its very nature baffles the rational mind, causing it to struggle toward spiritual awakening. This can be seen, for instance, in the play *Oedipus*, in which the king is given the answer outright in prophecy, but because it is encoded, being an utterance from an Oracle, he is unable to understand its implications and meaning until much later, after much personal agony and intense struggle – through which he is made wise.

Prophecy, then, must always be incomprehensible on a purely rational level, arising as it does from the transcendent. And so once again we can see evidence of the same Western historical arc down toward the material, marked by the literalist 'predictions' of 'seers' which began to appear perhaps most notably after the Renaissance, but culminating in the proliferation of modern 'seers' of a 'new age' – it need hardly be said that these exist, as it were, at the very polar opposite of true prophecy. For true prophecy defies the rational mind, acting as a spur towards spiritual awakening, drawing one upward, as it were, whereas predictions sow anxiety and discord and are confined to the temporal realm: from this indication alone it is clear in which directions each of these tends, prophecy being a warning to avert spiritual catastrophe; prediction referring only to the world of events and phenomena. An instance of the former can be seen in the writings of Abraham ben Samuel Abulafia, who lived in twelfth-century Spain and whose visionary writings – and mode of recitation of the Divine Name – acted to revive the primordial element latent in Qabalism, at least for a time, while the most dangerous instance of the latter can be seen in those today who, 'inspired' by those forces which led to the modern veneration of 'progress' and 'evolution,' predict a 'new age' in which 'science' and 'magic' merge – for this 'new man' must exist as we have seen at the very opposite pole from tradition, being in fact its inverted or infernal image.[18] Of course, from a cyclical perspective such an inversion is necessary in order to 'exhaust' man's lowest potentialities in order that the cycle may begin anew and 'purified' with a primordial, golden era.[19] And it is in the context of this primordial era that other phenomena – principally those of invisibility and telepathy – may also be understood.

For in terms of the primordial era, in which man and nature

are in harmonic union, such phenomena are not 'supernatural' – rather they are the natural result of an existence much freer of the 'interference' of habit energy and egotism than our own. To illustrate this, let us first examine the phenomenon of 'invisibility.'

What is it, after all, which makes us noticeable amongst others? Clearly it is our persona – that is, the accumulated residue of mechanical existence, or habit energy. Hence, when we walk through a crowd and are recognized, it is because key aspects of our habitual behaviour – our habitual gait, stance or manner or speech – are visible. And consequently, when this habitual energy is attenuated – either through religious practice or through the natural harmony of primordial man – then the result is a relative invisibility: that is, *one leaves no trace*.

And so one indication of the 'primordiality' of a culture is the extent to which it 'leaves no trace' in the physical world.

That this is the real meaning of invisibility was retained in the West, albeit in analogical language, until relatively recently, as indicated in John Aubrey's *Remaines of Gentilisme and Judaisme*, where the following 'receit' for invisibility is found:

> Take on Midsummer night, a xii, Astrologically when all the Planets are above the earth, a serpent and kill him and skin him, and dry it in the shade, and bring it to a powder. Hold it in your hand and you will be invisible. This receit is in Johannes de Florentia, (a Rosy-Crucian) a book in 8° high Dutch. A dr. Ridgely the Physician has it and told me of it.[20]

What are we to make of such instructions? Though literally they are absurd, analogically – in terms of the Hermetic cosmology which we have been following – they are quite comprehensible. For 'the snake' is a reference to the mercurial ego, which must be killed and skinned – that is, its illusory nature exposed, after which it is ground to a powder (its habit energy broken down). It then must be held in the hand – that is, the power released must infuse daily life and be controlled. The summer solstice is the midpoint of the solar year, the equilibrium point of the sun, moon and planets, which refers to the equilibrium of the magus as well. It implies the establishment of the horizontal, spiritual harmonization which is a prerequisite for any spiritual ascent – and hence harks directly back to the harmonizing nature of the primordial culture discussed earlier, though by the time John Aubrey wrote, the understanding of the necessity for harmonizing the 'influences' in the soul was very much 'lost knowledge.'

In fact, invisibility is very much the state in which traditional cosmology today appears: to those who are aware only of physical existence it is indeed invisible, just as from the most limited view of all, those who have transcended habit energy – like the cultures which further that transcendence – also seem to 'be as if they were not.'[21]

But as Novalis once wrote: the audible clings to the inaudible, and the visible to the invisible. And in truth the latter can well be said to have more 'reality' than the former!

Seen in this way, invisibility is not a childish trick played by the magus – as it is portrayed, for instance, in Marlowe's *Faust*, when the good doctor becomes invisible wholly to play japes upon the Pope.[22] Rather, it is the sign and symbol of the way true magic works: as a manifestation of the attenuation of habit – energy and ego for the benefit of others.

Ultimately, then, 'invisibility' is but a natural manifestation of the recognition that all is Mind, for to become invisible is in fact a kind of demonstration that *all* – including the body and the ego – is illusory.[23]

And this is likewise true for that phenomena which we term 'telepathy.' For like 'invisibility,' telepathy is only inexplicable if one thinks in terms of duality, of 'I' and 'thou,' and when that illusion of duality is transcended, telepathy becomes quite plausible, for with the transcendence of habit energy, the illusory barriers which separate us from the world also 'drop away.' Since each individual is in reality a microcosm, it is not inexplicable that he should be able to perceive thoughts or events irrespective of distance, for all things converge upon, reflect in, each individual already, if he could but perceive it.

It is the ego that conceives of time and space as real, as divided. This can be shown by the simple illustration of a line and a point. The ego, the point, 'conceives' of itself as standing outside the flow of time, which it perceives as a linear movement from past to future. But the more the point realizes itself to be a part of – and draws closer to – the center of the line, the more this ego 'drops away' and the more the flow of the line is perceived to be oneself. From the exact center of the line, everything – past and future – resolves into the circle of wholeness, the full moon: all occurs at once, and not at all. With this in mind, both 'telepathy' and 'invisibility' become comprehensible, both being a 'reflection' of the realization that space and time, in Mind, are illusory: that is, neither real nor not real.

Thus we can see why it is that within the primordial culture such phenomena can only be natural, since at the beginning of a human cycle there is virtually no residual habit energy, the individual is relatively free of disturbing, confused thoughts, and is very much attuned to the rhythms and harmonies of the cosmos and to all beings. In this, the Golden Age, one cannot so much speak of 'telepathy' – which implies a 'sender' and 'receiver' or a duality – but rather of the simultaneous arising of harmonious thoughts and intentions.

Yet not all 'supernatural' phenomena have simply receded and become remote by virtue of our present distance from primordial culture – certain phenomena, because of that historical arc downwards of which we spoke earlier, have taken on negative aspects simply due to the absence of anyone to 'channel' them properly. For after all, in the traditional philosophies of both Neoplatonism and Buddhism, the cause of error is but ignorance.

And clearly one such phenomenon is 'spontaneous combustion.'

FIRE AND THE INVERSION OF MAGIC

'Spontaneous combustion' is a phenomena which occurs seemingly at random and with no external cause: people simply burst into flames and disintegrate, charring from within. There was, for instance, a case in Britain in which a man fell asleep for four days in his car, and when he awoke found himself charred, as if the burn marks had proceeded from the inside of his body outward.[24] These cases suggest of course the there is a force or capacity within each individual for the generation of an inner heat, and if it is not 'channeled' in the proper way – as in Tibetan *gtummo*, or fire-yoga – then it breaks out on its own, causing damage like a storm over an area with no magus, no one to quiet it.

That this is so is corroborated by the esoteric science of

gtummo practiced in Buddhist Tibet, where it arose in part out of physical necessity due to the bitter cold, hermits there often living in a cave through the harsh winter wearing only a thin cotton shirt.

According to the *Yoga of the Psychic Heat*,[25] edited by Dr Evans-Wentz, the visualizations preceding the production of psychic heat begin with the visualization of oneself as the deity Vajra-yogini, one of the divine consorts who carries a divine sword, is adorned with bloody human skulls, and stands atop a human corpse. The student is to visualize himself as transparent, vacuous, growing ever larger until he encompasses the universe, and ever smaller until he is less than a sesamun seed. After a number of other exercises, including visualizing all the pores of the body as wrathful, flaming deities, one begins the Fundamental practice, alluded to as follows:

> By retaining in the psychic centers the vital-force;
> Something akin to heat is produced at first;
> Secondly, blissfulness is experienced;
> Thirdly, the mind assumes its natural state;
> Then the forming of thoughts ceases automatically,
> And phenomena, appearing like smoke, mirage, and fireflies,
> And something resembling the light of dawn
> And something resembling a cloudless sky are seen.

As we can see, the phenomenon achieved – in this case the inner fire – is but one byproduct of a much greater and deeper inner transformative process. The inner fire, then, is a phenomena closely connected with alchemy, largely in regard to the fire at the base of the alembic, or distilling vessel – a symbolic representation of the human body. Although this will be discussed more intently in Part III, suffice it to say that while the inner fire is a byproduct of the meditative spiritual transmutation, on an analogical level it also refers to the 'heat' produced by onepointed concentration, so that in a sense it is simultaneously cause and effect, so to speak. In alchemical terms it can be described as follows: the alchemist takes within himself the 'visualized' breath and saliva and, in a state of tranquillity, transmutes them into mercury and sulphur, which are to be united in cinnabar – mercurial sulfate – in the 'alchemical furnace' beneath the diaphragm (in Chinese: the Court of the Yellow Emperor). The more this mixture is heated

– much like diamonds – the purer and clearer it becomes. Though the process described is Chinese spiritual alchemy, it is remarkably close to that of the European alchemist Paracelsus, whose system was also based upon the union of Mercury and Sulphur under heat, under onepointed concentration and the inner fire.

For, after all, fire is the symbol of transformation *par excellence*; it is only through fire that even metal can be transformed. In terms of the analogy of the candle given earlier, the inner fire symbolizes the point of transmutation from below – where the flame appears as Divine Wrath – to above, from which vantage point it is recognized to be oneself, by which one is consumed in order to give light.[26] From this point of view, even hell itself is not ultimately 'punishment' but is in fact a manifestation of Divine Compassion and 'exists' as a 'place' of purification and transmutation. 'Spontaneous combustion,' then, is the 'inner fire,' 'uncontrolled.'

We can thus see that magic is inextricably, simultaneously literal and analogical, being at once symbol and reality – and this is all the more true the closer one is in spirit at least to 'primordiality' and man's first emergence in this world. And the same can be said of all phenomena which we label 'supernatural' – that is, in their pure form they are at once 'real' and symbolic manifestations of the human place within the cosmos, acting therefore for the good (for the spiritual liberation) of all sentient beings. Yet in our present era this is manifestly not the case, for today even in the few remaining 'primitive' cultures or tribes the sorcerer or magus is hated and feared, an attitude which signifies the exact inversion of the traditional place which magic held within the primordial world. And so, before we can conclude our discussion of magic and primordiality, we must examine the nature of a phenomena which virtually recapitulates this inversion of the traditional: we turn to a phenomena termed 'bearwalking.'

'Bearwalking' is a phenomenon closely aligned with that of spontaneous combustion, not only because it is accompanied by the emergence of a literal, physical fire, but also because it represents the negative manifestation of forces which in a normal culture are channeled into beneficent uses.

'Bearwalking' is generally agreed to occur as follows: an Indian tribesman (in northern North America) conceives a dislike for one of his or her fellows and one night, if he is a 'bearwalker,' he goes outside, travels a great distance as a ball of fire, wreaks havoc upon his enemy, and returns home. The 'bearwalker' is, needless to say, feared above all others, and one can easily imagine the destructive cultural consequences of that fear – for no one knows who else might be such a one: it might be a relative or friend.[27] And so paranoia reigns.

This is precisely what has happened, not only among northern tribes, but even amongst the Hopis, where for some years now they have lived in fear of one another, afraid that even their own family members might be sorcerers who must, as a result of their immense past evil, kill relatives in order to prolong their own lives.[28] Such a situation is indisputably the exact inversion of the traditional culture, in which magic acts to unify, to draw upward and harmonize all beings – for here, in the present era, it acts to break apart, to spread fear and confusion and destruction.

It is clear, as we have noted elsewhere, that this inversion of the traditional place of magic must take place in order that the cycle might complete itself, in order that absolute dispersion and disintegration might 'exhaust itself' in an utter parody of the primordial world, and nowhere can this be more clearly seen than in the cases of 'bearwalking,' of which 'spontaneous combustion' is but a weak prelude. For the latter involves merely ignorance of fundamental laws, but 'bearwalking' involves the actual *inversion* of the primordial culture, so that rather than drawing together and upward, the magus is a sorcerer, who acts to spread fear and destruction, tearing the culture apart from within. But the question remains: why is this, among those who, until very recently, were the closest to primordiality?

For after all, both the Eskimo and the North American Indians lived in a world in which the division of self and other, man and nature, was far less distinct than in the modern age: the earth, the herbs, the animals all eloquently radiated the Great Spirit, the celestial realm.[29] The answer is suggested by the ease with which the modern era overswept the traditional cultures of the Orient: that the immediate exposure to that which developed in the West over many centuries has a much more profound impact on a culture still retaining any degree of primordiality, causing it to 'leap forward' through all the phases of the cycle much more quickly. But because of the suddenness of this accelerated downward arc, some elements of the traditional, the primordial, must still remain, just as in Mahayana Buddhist representations even of *Narakas*, or hells, there is a Buddha – for even the darkest of illusions must remain finally that: an illusion.

In any case, leaving aside the connection between the 'psychism' and 'neoshamanism' of our present era and the phenomena of 'bearwalking' – and their respective destructive effects upon that which remains of primordiality – we can nonetheless begin to recognize the abyss which separate. the present era from the primordial, the magic of the Golden Age from the sorcery of our own, and we can begin to re-member our own place and true function in the cosmos as harmonizer, as the one being in whom all the realms might be realized and through whom all nature might be fulfilled: we can begin to realize who we really are.

For after all, truth can only be known in contradistinction from error, just as reality can only be seen when illusion has been vanquished – and so too it must be that in the darkest era of the darkest age we must, paradoxically, be closest to the purest light, if we could but see it.

And so we turn from the lowest to the highest, we turn from one end of the spectrum back toward the other: we turn, before we conclude, to the primordial teaching of the journey of the soul.

THE JOURNEY OF THE SOUL TOWARD LIBERATION

Strictly speaking we cannot speak of a 'journey of the soul,' since from an ultimate point of view all terms denoting a separate individuality must be null, referring as they do to the realm of manifestation. But if we keep in mind that such terms are merely provisional and that, as Origen said, the 'soul' arises from and is resolved into Mind in a 'journey' which is in no wise temporal, then we may use them in the same way that the ancients used them: as convenient devices to further under-standing of that about which nothing may finally be spoken at all. Nonetheless, one must remember that such terms bespeak a dualism which in a state of primordiality must necessarily be resolved into a principal unity, a state in which dualistic terms no longer obtain. With this in mind we can begin to approach those two works in Western tradition which use these very terms to point toward that state of primordiality: Plato's *Republic* and Cicero's *On the Commonwealth*.

It is no coincidence that the clearest explications of the 'journey of the soul' in ancient Greece and Rome are found in the chief political writings of that era, and in fact form the culmination of those writings. For as we have seen, all within the primordial culture acts to 'magically' further the liberation of those within its realm, and since both Plato's and Cicero's works point directly toward the traditional culture[30] as an inherent *locus*, it is hardly surprising that both works should climax with the 'myth of Er' and the 'dream of Scipio' respectively. Just as in the *Republic* the 'myth of Er' stands as a signpost pointing to the ultimate impermanence of human existence and the need to reform not only the city without but the city within, so too the 'dream of Scipio' implies that all cultural and political realms must be subsumed to, and a reflection of, the greater cosmological meaning of human existence.[31]

Both the 'myth of Er' and the 'dream of Scipio' are accounts given by men who have ascended, during life, to the supracelestial realm and there witnessed the primordial cosmology, only to return to earth in order to tell the living of 'that which follows death.' In the 'myth of Er,' Plato tells of Er, the son of Armenius, who for twelve days apparently died and went upon a 'journey of a thousand years' in which he entered a great meadow upon which were encamped the sullied spirits of the dead rising from earth along with the clean spirits descending from Heaven. In that place, said Er, they gathered to speak about the world on earth and the one in heaven; there it was that they heard of the punishments for evil deeds done upon earth.

After seven days in the meadow, the spirits had to go onward to a great spindle, a line of Light purer than the rainbow, of all colours and extending through heaven and earth. Upon this line turn all the forms and spindles of destiny and necessity, and all the planets. There the spirits were given by the fates their lots for future destinies. They were able to choose, but most were blinded by their past actions and so chose unwisely, becoming beggars or criminals. When all had chosen their future lives, they went on to the plain of forgetfulness, where they were forced to drink of the river of unmindfulness, and in proportion as they drank they forgot all truth and light. Er, of course, was not allowed to drink. In the middle of the night there was a thunderstorm and in an instant they were driven forth like shooting stars to the circumstances of their births – but Er awoke to find himself upon the funeral pyre.

There is so much in the 'myth of Er' – as in the 'dream of Scipio,' both being manifestations of the Mystery tradition – that one could hardly hope to elucidate it in a volume. Nonetheless, several things may be noted. First, we might point out the similarity to what is commonly called Eastern thought. We have here the inevitable blinding effect of *karma* – the web of cause and effect which drives one to rebirth and which determines one's place in life through ignorance or forgetfulness, the chief evil[32] in traditional cosmology both Buddhist and Platonic. We have the three worlds – supracelestial, celestial and earthly – joined in a spindle of blinding light about which all things turn. In Buddhist teaching this spindle corresponds to Mount Sumeru, the 'mountain' at the center of the worlds. We have forgetfulness and unmindfulness as the cause of inevitable human suffering – ignorance of the Divine. We have the planetary correspondences and colours. The twelve days of Er which last 'one thousand years' point to the attribution of longevity to sages[33] – for the soul which has ascended above the timeline into the Pure Land, a relative or virtual immortality is achieved, in that temporal limitation no longer exists.

In short, in both the 'myth of Er' and the 'dream of Scipio' it is quite evident that the supposed abyss between 'Eastern' and 'Western' thought is not nearly so great as has been commonly maintained – for in their origins they are and must be one. Indeed, the present differences derive almost solely from the fact that in Buddhism the original, primordial teaching was preserved and transmitted, whereas the Hermetic teaching of Plato and Cicero was obscured and abandoned, so that virtually nothing from the Orphic, Eleusinian, Dionysian or other Mystery schools, to which undoubtedly Plato and Cicero were to some extent privy, was maintained.

In any case, we can approach the primordial teaching of the

'journey of the soul' on three different levels, as it were, according to metaphysical profundity. The highest 'point of view' is that expressed in the Tibetan *Bardo Thötröl*, or *Book of the Dead*, in which the hearer is constantly reminded that he is none other than the Light – Mind – and that all his visions, from the highest celestial realms downward into manifestation, are but illusion.[34] From this primordial point of view one cannot speak of either soul or journey, nor even of liberation. On the 'second level' – from a more limited point of view – we have the teaching found in the 'myth of Er' which, if followed, can bestow a virtual immortality, but which does not lead to liberation, being a 'provisional' understanding which only points toward the original, principal unity. On the 'third level' we have the most literal point of view, in which the 'soul' is imagined to have actually 'journeyed' or to have 'appeared' in a number of places, and it is at this level that we can see evidence at once of the two poles or extremes of history – it is here that our discussion turns full circle, and we can conclude.

For in terms of the primordial unity, the Golden Age, as we have seen, one cannot properly speak in dualistic terms: spirit and matter, man and nature, celestial and temporal – all are resolved in a condition of harmonious interpenetration, and in such an age the tales of the Taoist Ko Hung of his uncle who could 'appear' in a dozen places at once to astonish guests are not incomprehensible, or even whimsical, but refer instead to a time beyond time, to the primordial dawn of humanity in which magic is natural, and all nature is magical. At the other end of the spectrum, however, one finds the literal belief in a 'soul' which 'journeys' in the temporal realm – a delusion which could only arise in an era in which all must be related to the material and temporal – and a delusion which can only lead one downward into the abyss of absolute dissolution.[35]

Yet from the provisional point of view we can see that even this – the greatest of all delusions – is necessary in order that the cycle might be 'completed,' in order that all delusion might 'exhaust itself' like clouds dispersing before a Sun, and the Golden Age might manifest itself once again.

And from the ultimate point of view, one can speak neither of path nor of one who traverses the path, neither seeker nor sought, neither delusion nor enlightenment. For as it is written in the *Prajnaparamita Sutra*:

Form is no other than Sunyata,
Sunyata is no other than Form;
Form is exactly Sunyata, Sunyata exactly Form;
Feeling, thought, discrimination, perception
Are likewise like this . . .
All phenomena are Sunyata:
Not born, not destroyed,
Not stained, not pure,
Without loss, without gain;
So in Sunyata there is no form,
No feeling, thought, discrimination, perception;
No eye, ear, nose, tongue, body, mind;
No sight, sound, smell, taste, touch, object;
No world of sight, no world of consciousness;
No ignorance and no end to ignorance . . .
No old age and death and no end to old age and death;
No suffering, no craving, no extinction, no Path;
No wisdom, no attainment, nothing to be attained.

It is with this realization that the true magic — the recognition of that which is beyond all limiting conceptions,
including that of 'soul' — begins in earnest.

PART III

ALCHEMY

Alchemy, like magic, has long been dismissed as a futile and primitive quest for power and wealth. But alchemy is no more the blundering attempts of misguided fools to find a means to make gold than magic is the naive expression of superstitious people lacking in the reason and common sense we in the modern world are assumed to possess. Rather, alchemy, like magic, is above all the transformation of objects, colours and actions into signs and symbols of progress on the inner journey of spiritual transmutation. For were alchemy and magic but a dead end, they would have long since disappeared – but they persist, in attenuated form, as even the presence of this book attests; they persist because they are the eternal expression of the spiritual regeneration of man, and can never be obliterated.

It is because this is so that alchemists, Eastern and Western, despite widely varying cultures, can agree with such remarkable regularity on the nature and steps in alchemical and magical ritual. It is most striking to read the quintessential Western alchemist, Paracelsus, and then turn to Ko Hung, the Taoist alchemist of fourth-century AD China, and to Jabir ibn Hayyan, the tenth-century Arabic alchemist, and find that each of them corresponds in teaching with very little variation. This unanimity is above all due to the fact that alchemy is the mirror of eternal principles and stages in spiritual transmutation, and so must ever be one. But in addition, there is evidence that alchemy followed a path of transmission from the Near East both West and East, into Europe and China.

Titus Burckhardt, in his study of alchemy, traces the transmission of alchemy from before the rise of the Egyptian civilization, through to Alexandria, where it was codified and placed in the largely written form in which it was transmitted both to the West, through the Greeks, and to the East.[1] On the other hand, the pure form of inner alchemy which has survived in Tibet up to this day may well be a bastion of the original proto-Indo-European civilization.[2] In any case, the likelihood of transmission from one place to another derives from the fact that magic and alchemy – and the spiritual transmutation which they represent – is orally transmitted from master to disciple. That which accumulated in books is merely the other manifestation of what must be a living spiritual tradition and that is why, prior to the Alexandrian writings, there are virtually no alchemical manuscripts, even though the amulets and other remnants of the Egyptian times attest to alchemy's existence. Alchemy was not codified at that time because it was still wholly living, and did not need to be written down. Regardless of whether there was a specific oral tradition of alchemy which travelled East and West from Egypt, or whether the teachings which produced alchemy arose spontaneously as divine revelation on each continent, both the fact of their remarkable unity, and of the necessity of their being passed on by an accomplished master, are certain. It is to the particularities of that unity that we now turn.

The very word alchemy illustrates the universal nature of the art, for it may be variously traced to the Arabic *al-kimiyya* (to transmute) or to the Egyptian *keme*, which refers to the black earth to be transmuted, or to the Greek *chyma*, or 'smelting.' The intertwined nature of these words and meanings points toward the nature of alchemy, which exists on several levels simultaneously. For the essence of alchemy is to use base material symbols – such as Sulphur, Mercury and Salt – to illustrate the most recondite spiritual experiences. Hence, in its very nature, alchemy expresses the highest unity, to which Mahayana Buddhism refers as the 'inseparability of nirvana and samsara,' the polar union of the ultimate spiritual bliss and the phenomenal world. The moon is the sign of this union in both Taoism and Buddhism, in that while it is the symbol of tides and generation, of imprisonment in samsara, it is also a reflection of Light, perfect and round.

In alchemy, as in magic, the spiritual and the physical are never conceived as opposites, but rather the physical is seen as a reflection of its spiritual essence. Matter is seen as the mirror upon which Mind reflects. Then, too, the use of physical principles to illustrate the highest forms of spiritual transmutation is a paradox intended by its very nature to blunt the merely rational mind, much as a koan in Zen Buddhism, by creating an intense mass of doubt and questioning, builds to such a point within the mind of the seeker as to burst through its bonds of ego, transforming habit energy into spiritual energy.

In all forms of alchemy, this instant – the realization of the Great Work – appears as an instant of thunderous illumination in which both oneself and the world are transformed. But such a moment can only be realized after many years of intense and devoted study and practice. Thus, as in magic, the actual transubstantiation of base metals into gold is the ultimate byproduct of an inner process, not an end in itself, which would make it a profane, egotistically motivated desire and thus inherently bound to fail.

In any case, there are a number of forms, terms and substances which recur in alchemy, terms and principles which transcend the various languages in which they occur. The first and most prominent of these must be the philosopher's Stone, that enigmatic *lapis alchemicum* which has the power to transmute any base material into its exalted form. There, the mere fact that attainment of this Stone is necessary before one can turn base metal into gold suggests that the same relationshp which governs magic is true in alchemy: the discovery of the Philosopher's Stone is the true aim, and the transmutation of lead into gold is a possible byproduct, just as the phenomenon of magic is the byproduct of the emptying of self. What, then, is the nature of this philosophical stone?

Arnauld de Villeneuve, in his *Commentaire sur Hortulain*, said that

> the mixture of three things is called the Blessed Stone –
> mineral, animal and vegetable, because it has no proper

name: mineral because it is compounded of mineral things, vegetable because it lives and vegetates, and animal because it has a body, soul and spirit like animals.[3]

And, said Nicholas Valois, to clarify the matter, 'it is a stone of Great Virtue, and it is called a stone, and it is not a Stone.' Although it may not at first appear to be so, in these two quotations we find the true definition of the Philosophical Stone. But to draw out that meaning, we must first examine the trinity of alchemical components from which the Stone is created. For in both Western and Eastern alchemy, there are but three principle elements, elements which are not to be taken so much as atomic elements – for traditional Neoplatonic and Buddhist theosophies had long ago rejected the atomistic reductionism of the materialists, in favor of affirming the existence of Mind alone.

Once this is understood, the underlying cosmology of alchemy becomes clear, for then the essence of existence is seen not as random atoms, but *as consciousness. The central premise of alchemy is not to delineate a mere division of the elements, but rather to describe the levels and aspects of consciousness of which matter is but a reflection.* Once this fundamental shift in understanding is grasped, the nature of alchemy becomes quite clear. For if all existence is recognized as aspects of consciousness, then there is no dichotomy between the transmutation of self and transmutation of actual elements: all are emanations of Mind.

The central dilemma in interpreting alchemical writings has always been the dichotomy between the physical and the spiritual. And the general assumption has been that the alchemists, by transmuting base metals in a laboratory, somehow mysteriously managed to transform themselves, and that in this way the dichotomy has been explained away. However, this explanation is wholly inverted, wholly specious. For the basic understanding upon which alchemy is based can hardly be as superficial as that: if it were, either everyone who worked with metals would become a saint, or alchemy would long since have disappeared. It is the transmutation of self which precedes that of metals, not the other way round. In this way alone is the dichotomy of physical and spiritual resolved.

For this reason, the alchemists were constantly warning that

ALCHEMY

the Mercury of which they spoke was not common mercury but
something else, that the Gold of which they spoke was not a
common gold, but another and more lustrous thing, from
which gold – the metal – was descended and of which it was a
reflection. What then did the alchemists mean by the terms
Gold, Sulphur, Mercury and Salt, if not the simple elements
themselves? They meant to illustrate aspects of Mind.

If the central teaching of Mahayana Buddhism – that all
existence is an aspect and reflection of Mind and therefore has
no inherent reality of its own – is taken as the premise upon
which alchemy was based, then the fundamental meaning of
alchemy becomes apparent. Alchemy, then, is a transcendent
fusion of religious, philsophical and scientific knowledge – a
theosophy – which describes not the base elements of nature,
but rather the spiritual components and principles, the aspects
of the celestial world and pure consciousness from which the
base elements are descended, and which they mirror. Hence the
combination and realization of these principles is realization of
the higher essences of Reality itself.

That this is so is made clear by the epitome of Western
alchemists, Paracelsus himself. Said Paracelsus:

We have before said that the primal matter consists in its
mother, just as if in a bag, and that it is composed of three
ingredients meeting in one. But there are as many varieties of
Mercury, Salt and Sulphur as there are different fruits in
minerals. For a different Sulphur is to be found in lead, iron
and gold; in sapphires and other gems . . . and in different
salts; likewise a different Salt is found in metal salts, and so
on. So, too, is it with Mercury: one kind exists in gems,
another in metals.

Finally, said Paracelsus, 'All these matters does that one and
the same Nature at once embrace in one. . . . This is the way of
safety from below to above.'

It is clear that if, as Paracelsus said, there is a different
Sulphur to be found in lead than in iron and gold, he is talking
about a system very much different from the two-dimensional
chart of elements in present use, for it is certain that Mercury,
Sulphur and Salt as we know them are not at all present in
most minerals and substances. But Paracelsus was not examining the world from an atomistic, two-dimensional, and ever

109

more divisive point of view. Rather, he was, with his Mercury, Sulphur and Salt adding a third and deeper level to phenomenal existence. He is adding the third dimension: depth, so the world may be seen whole, through to its Origin. That third dimension is none other than consciousness.

The three elements of Paracelsus are none other than aspects of consciousness, and the more one perceives them in all things, the more one is led back to the One from which they arise and to which they return. The natural world is, through alchemical theosophy and inquiry, being traced back to its roots, its Source in the celestial realm of Essences, seen here as the conscious principles of Mercury, Salt and Sulphur, and finally back to the One of Nature, which is Paracelsus's term for Mind. For this reason the alchemists said that one must first find the *prima materia*, the matrix, mater, or mother, in which all phenomena are united. That matrix appears to us as Void, since it is the celestial realm and unseen by the individual trapped in the temporal, illusory ego, but the Void is in Reality the source of all being, from which emanate the trinity of principles – the Trinity of aspects of consciousness – and then, below them, the material realm.

The reason that this alchemical understanding is so difficult for the modern mind to grasp is that it does not regard matter and spirit as a duality at all, but rather all are emanations of Mind, vibrations and harmonies at different levels.

Therefore, when an alchemist explains how to combine Sulphur, Mercury and Salt in the proper proportion, he is neither speaking in rudely literal terms – as the puffers thought – nor is he speaking in wholly symbolic and psychic terms – as the psychologisers thought. Rather, for the alchemist, all is composed of, and is a reflection of Mind and Consciousness, and there is no dilemma whatever in speaking of combining Mercury, Sulphur and Salt, because these are an empirical description of the basic conscious principles of which the universe is a mirror. The modern mind seeks to divide ever further in order to understand; the alchemist seeks to unite, to find the underlying principles of harmony, and to follow them back to their Source in Mind. Inasmuch as modern physics progresses will it come to resemble the alchemical understanding of existence.

For, as Paracelsus said, 'that is the way of safety from below to above.' In other words, alchemy is above all a purification of consciousness and of awareness, a burning away of the dross of ego in order that the pure light of the celestial realm may be manifested.

If one takes the Trinity of principles to be elements of consciousness, with what, then, are they associated? According to Paracelsus, all colours proceed from the Salt of Nature, all substance is exhibited by Sulphur, and all virtue and arcana proceed from Mercury. But to clarify the matter: in general, Sulphur is the masculine principle, Mercury is feminine, and Salt is the crystalline which conjoins them. These are not rules, but tendencies. Sulphur is indicative of the male principle because it is active: it flares, giving light, when burned. Sulphur is the chemical manifestation of the yellow, solar principle; it is dangerous when not balanced by Mercury, the lunar principle. Mercury is one below silver on the periodic table, confirming their traditional association as lunar principles through colour and character. Indeed, alchemically, Mercury is the inconstant, mutable form of silver just as sulphur is the mutable form of gold. Again, these are neither literal, nor psychological divisions, but rather are eternal principles manifested inasmuch as ego and habit energy are broken down and transmuted. Alchemically, this breaking down is represented by the finding of the *prima materia*, the primal continuum beyond existence, obscured by the illusion of ego, but common to all sentient beings, all phenomena.

The relationship is shown by the diagram on page 112 of the two triangles joined at the apex. Interestingly, when they are merged they form Solomon's Seal, that best known of magic figures, and sign of completion.

In this regard, it is interesting to note that if animal blood is allowed exposure to air, it will rapidly turn to sulphuric acid as the mercuric or vaporous lunar principle – water – evaporates. This suggests that original division with which we began this discussion, the division of Arnauld de Villeneuve who said that the Philosophic Stone was to be disclosed by the union of mineral, vegetable and animal realms. These realms corres-pond, of course, to Salt – the crystalline, geometric realm of mineral Form – Mercury, which is the lunar, vegetable realm – and Sulphur, which is the component of animal blood remaining when blood is left to the elements, signifying its

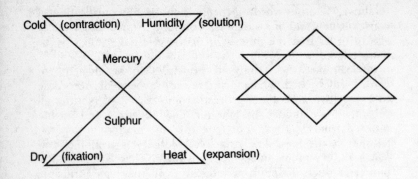

XII   The Seal of Solomon

solar, animal connections. In esoteric terms, these three
correspond to the three pillars of Zen Buddhism, Taoism and
alchemy. Salt – the Form – is sitting in zazen meditation.
Mercury represents the circulation of the breath – the
clarification, purification and pacifiation of the thoughts which
subside in Breath, the vegetable realm. And Sulphur represents
the influx of transcendent knowledge, or gnosis, the flash of
pure Light and awareness. Thus the Great Work is precisely as
de Villeneuve said: it is the process of uniting the three realms,
the three celestial principles – mineral, vegetable and animal, or
Salt, Mercury and Sulphur – within the microcosm of the
alchemist, within his athanor, his inner spiritual furnace.

These three celestial principles, then, are the suprarational
animating force that infills all the phenomenal world, so that
when the alchemist speaks of realizing and combining their
essences, he is in fact talking in very specific and descriptive
terms, not about the exoteric appearance of reality, but about
its higher Platonic Forms, which he realizes within himself until
finally he reaches that point which is the negation of all
existence and all perception, the negation of all created and
uncreated, that which cannot touch or be touched, that
ultimate center of Emptiness at the heart of the Cloud of
Unknowing, the Stone which is called a stone and yet is not a
Stone, that which can neither be named nor comprehended:
Mind.

This is a Mystery the depths of which can never be plumbed nor even imagined.

But it is a Mystery glimpsed though Fire. Not the destructive and impure fire of earth, but rather the Fire of concentrative meditation which purifies and unifies inasmuch as it breaks down habit energy and the illusion of the self. To achieve the proper degree and aspect of Fire is most difficult, as every alchemist will attest. The alchemist Pontanus, in his *Empire*, said that his attempts at completing the Great Work went astray over 200 times before he learned of the true Philosophic Fire. Like the water, or Mercury which must be of a kind which 'never wet the hands,' so the fire must be of a kind which never burned upon earth: it must be within.

The alchemists assure the seeker continually – pointing, as it were, directly at the sense of the matter – that the Work must take place within one vessel and is but one operation. Philalethes, for instance, says that the 'terms distillation, sublimation, calcination, assation, neverberation, dissolution, descension and coagulation are no more than one sole and single operation performed in one and the same vase.' (In Enarration methodica trium Gebri verborum.) In addition, as if to confirm the obvious place of the transmutation, all references to the Principles are in the possessive: it is always *our* Water, *our* Sulphur, *our* Salt, and not the elements the vulgar know by that name. In other words, the vase which contains the Orphic Egg (the aludel in which transmutation takes place) is none other than our own body, and the principles are nowhere if not within us – as are the very constellations, as Elias Ashmole pointed out in his *Theatrum Chemicum Brittanicum.*[4]

That fire is the central part of the transformative process is clear even in the earliest alchemical treatises known in Europe, one of which is known as the *Revelations of Morienus, Ancient Adept and Hermit of Jerusalem to Khalid Ibn Yazid Ibn Mu'Awiyya, King of the Arabs.*[5] After the admonition, in this work, that 'you should know that the earth and stone and all those things I have named, in which men trust, are false and come to no good name,' which refers to the Emptiness of which all things are formed, Morienus goes on to say that 'the whole key to the accomplishment of this operation is in the fire, with which the minerals are prepared and the bad spirits held back, and *with which the spirit and body are joined.* Fire is the true test of this entire matter.' And to make the matter yet more clear, Morienus continues, adding that the white vapour, or Virgin's Milk which the adept should manifest in the operation, is the tincture or spirit of the dead which has been withdrawn from the earth, and which the alchemist must manifest upon earth and marry with the body. The implication is, of course, that we are ourselves dead until this operation is completed within us.

How the operation is completed is graphically illustrated in the *Bibliotheca Chemica* of Manget, published in Paris in 1702, where an illustration shows two alchemists, one male and one female, kneeling on either side of an athanor, or furnace, in a room empty of paraphernalia, praying. The levels of the athanor are even with those of the chakras in the alchemists, so that the fire is at the base of the spine, with a funnel or triangle just above it, and above that the Orphic Egg, the crown of the head being vented. Directly above the two who are praying is the celestial world of which they are a reflection. On the left, above, is the winged feminine curial spirit; on the right, above, is the winged male sulphuric angel; above them is the Sun of existence, and between them is the androgynous Completion of the work, in the Orphic Egg, standing above the Sun and Moon to signify the ultimate Union with the Soul. The Soul is holding the five level cross, symbolizing the completion of the five major steps and the union of the five lower elements, as well as the union of male and female in the three principles of Mercury, Sulphur and Salt to make One in the ascent, the vertical line. All of these things, however, are dependent upon the fire which is in the base of the athanor, burning away the dross. That fire is the psychic heat of meditation, concentrated beneath the navel.

Without the fire of meditative awareness which joins spirit and body, alchemy does not exist.

Nicolas Valois, a fifteenth-century alchemist, said in his *Cinq Livres*, or *Five Lives*, 'the good God granted me this divine secret through my prayers and the good intentions I had of using it well; the science is lost if purity is lost.' The alchemists, then, were well aware that the only means to achievement of the Philosophic Stone of Emptiness was intense inner meditation, by which the soul is purified. Gold is a symbol of the soul in its purity because gold, the colour of the sun, is always inherently pure and purifiable, no matter how much dross is added, just as the soul of man is eternally pure, even though it may be clouded and darkened by entrapment in ego. The use of gold as a symbol for the soul is significant in that it means that the alchemists taught – to use Buddhist terminology – that the Buddhanature is inherent in every sentient being, pure and undefiled, if only one can realize it. Lead is a symbol of the darkness of the soul because of its density and impenetrability, and because its colour – grey – symbolizes the soul's submission to the realm of the moon, of generation and decay, of birth and death, of water. The transmutation of lead into gold, then, signified the introduction of the Sun into the realm of the Moon, transmuting and exalting it. However, the creation of gold in both Eastern and Western alchemy – spiritual gold – was not the completion of the Work. The Work was completed only with the union of Sun and Moon, of Sulphur and Mercury, in Cinnabar, the Elixir of Life. For it is only then, when the celestial realm beyond birth and death has been realized, that true life, life beyond this fleeting temporality, this physical dream, can begin.

Perhaps the best recapitulation of the various stages in the inner alchemical transformation is to be found in Edward Kelly's *Theatre of Terrestrial Astronomy*,[6] in which a concise summary of the steps and their associations with the planets is given. Kelly begins his discussion of alchemy with mention of the holy numbers three and four, which together make the seat of power, seven. The four – the square or cross – symbolizes the temporal earth, while the three, the triangle, symbolizes the Trinity of Eternal Principles, above which is the Duality, above which is the One. Kelly identifies the colours of the planets as depicted in the drawing by the colours of the rainbow. First is Saturn – black as the raven's head; next is Jupiter, who is white. Then Mars, who is red, and Venus, who is green, follow, after which is Mercury, who is black, white, red and green together. Finally there is the Silver of the Moon and the Gold of the Sun. Above these planets – above the King, Man – is the incomprehensible Trinity, or Triangle, enclosed in a circle and next to the Sun and Moon. What, then, is signified by these planets and colours?

The answer lies even in the title of the work: terrestrial

115

astronomy. For the only place on earth reflecting, containing, the microcosm of the stars is Man, and it is in Man that the astronomical – inner – observation and transmutation symbolized by the planets takes place. In other words, says Kelly, the alchemical transmutation must begin with Saturn, the black planet of putrefaction, for 'our whole magistery is based upon putrefaction; it can come to nothing unless it is putrefied.'[7] That putrefaction is, in terms of this discussion, the breaking down of the habit energy, of the accretions of ego and black attachments to matter. The inner conjunction, says Kelly, is of the three – body, soul and spirit – which must be made into one, for, as he adds, the soul is the bond of the spirit, as the body is the bond of the soul, and they can only be joined after putrefaction, *'for nothing can be improved if its form has not previously been utterly destroyed.'*

Saturn, then, is the darkest part of the material sphere: the realm of birth and death in which we are trapped. But, too, Saturn represents putrefaction, which is the process of cleansing the soul of its dross, a process that begins with the very realization that one is trapped in the realm of birth and death. The reason that Kelly states that our whole magistery is based upon putrefaction is that only in the material realm – only upon earth – can the alchemical transmutation take place.

As moisture dries, says Kelly – that is, as the reign of water, of birth and death, loses its hold upon us – the colours shifting within blackness give way to a stable white colour – *Jupiter*, which is a glimpse of the soul's purity. The blue-blackness of *Saturn*, though, gives way to the whiteness of *Jupiter* slowly, for a hot fire would burst the vessel. The transformation of the human soul is never instantaneous, for even in Zen Buddhism, which is known as the 'Sudden Path,' many years of ripening must take place before the instantaneous clarification known as *satori*, or enlightenment can come to pass. It can be no different in alchemy.

This white tincture of *Jupiter* known as the Virgin's Milk, or the White Queen, or the Elixir of Life, must be purified wholly before one can increase the fire of meditation yet further and transform her into the Mighty King, who is ruby red in colour. Just as the Black must become White in colour, so the White must then become Red. This red, associated with *Mars*, implies the most intense part of the spiritual struggle, for while the shift from black to white is polar, the shift from white to red is to a wholly new level, identified with the addition of Sulphur. The White Queen is the symbol of the purification of Quicksilver; the Red King is the symbol of purification of Sulphur, through Fire.

After these are completed, then arises the Green of *Venus* – Green being the polar opposite of Red. Whereas the Red is associated with the blood of the Lion, Green is the sign of the Lion or Dragon himself – the Lion symbolizing awe and fear as one approaches the Holiest. Green is the sign of the entry into the celestial realm, which in Sūfism is known as hūrqūlyā – the emerald vision.[8] Green is the sign that the silver-blue of Quicksilver and the Gold-yellow of Sulphur has been united in love: *Venus*.

This is very near the final stage, which is represented by the planet *Mercury*, nearest the *Sun* itself. *Mercury* is the sign in which the summation of all the colours attained so far are united: *Mercury* is black, blue, white, yellow, red and green combined. Beyond *Mercury* lies the incomparable Majesty of the *Sun* and *Moon* themselves, symbolized by the majestic Purple of Royalty which awaits all who travel to that height. This Purple is the sign of that royal nature within us which has been obscured – as the Gnostic *Song of the Pearl*[9] describes – by blindness, forgetfulness, and wandering in the Sodom of this world. But just as the royal Son who has forgotten his inheritance is sent a messenger who reminds him of his Eternal nature and his purpose on earth – to bring the Pearl, the Orphic Egg back to his Royal Parents – so too are we sent a messenger: the texts of alchemy, which are a reminder of our Eternal nature and show us the path through which our Royal heritage can be regained.

Though men like Paracelsus and Böehme have been reviled over the centuries, it is precisely such men who prove to be the Salt of the earth;[10] it is they who have shown and will show the way to unite the Mercury and Sulphur in order to recover the Eternal. It is ironic that these very men who were in fact storing up their treasure in the celestial realm were forever accused of doing the opposite, of seeking to create earthly riches. This, despite the warning of every alchemist worth his salt that the treasures he sought were in heaven. As Basilius Valentinus said:

All clamour aloud: We want to be Rich! Rich! Yes, you
desire wealth and say with Epicurus: Let us provide for our
bodies and leave our souls to take care of themselves. Even as
Midas in the fable, you wish to turn all things into gold. So
there are numerous people who seek this gold in Antinomy,
but since they do not care for God, and have cast far away
from them the love of their neighbor, they will look at the
horse's teeth of Antinomy forever without knowing a thing
of its age or quality. Like the wedding guests of Cana, they
may behold, but . . . know nothing.[11]

One of the reasons that Edward Kelly became notorious is
that he at one time was reputed to have asked Dr John Dee, the
prominent Elizabethan scholar and astrologer, to exchange
wives. Whether or not this is true, the tale underscores the aim
of alchemy, which is to realize the transient nature of earthly
existence, and the necessity for freedom from clinging and
aversion, the two faces of the ego. If a suggestion of that nature
were to come from a Tibetan *guru*, its intent would be to
liberate.[12] This is the same suprarational reason that the
Prophet Muhammed – upon whom be peace – said that cats
were clean, while dogs were not. Cats are free from clinging;
dogs are a symbol of desire and longing, fury and aversion.
Kelly may well have been, with such a suggestion, not merely
flouting conventional morality, but rather seeking to show Dee
beyond the morass of dualism, of right and wrong. And it very
much appears that he was able to do so, for in his private
journal, Dee recorded the enigmatic notation that 'on this day
did E.K. reveal to me the Great Work, God be praised!' And, as
Dee said in his *Monas Hieroglyphica*, from that day forward
they went forth to 'sing praises to God and to preach the Thrice
Mighty because he had given them so much wisdom, and
power and so great an Empire over all other creatures.'

According to traditional Islamic cosmology – in which
alchemy was retained during its period of eclipse in the West –
minerals themselves are living within the earth, being the
product of the masculine seed impregnating the feminine earth.
Minerals are growing children beneath the surface, children
who arise when they have matured enough to aid the
development of pure life – the saint – upon earth. Minerals,
according to Jabir ibn Hayyan, the best known Arabic

alchemist, are not only alive, but have feelings and intentions just as do all living things. These intentions, however, are known only to God. Their purpose is always to benefit the highest of beings upon earth – as indeed all living things are created to do. In this we can see an exoteric application of alchemical and hermetic understanding, allowing us to glimpse that which draws together and guides all traditional civilizations. For in the traditional understanding of the cosmos, all human activity is organized around the Pole of human existence – those who have realized the nature of Reality.

Minerals, vegetables, animals, the soil, the water – all is united by the common purpose: to serve and to be uplifted by man, the microcosm, who alone is capable of realizing the Divine. In this way alchemy becomes a means of, a vision of, unifying human society under the realization of its true purpose, annihilating the present chaos as light annihilates the dark. As Jacob Böehme said: nothing exists for man as animal. Everything exists solely for man to become Angel.

The realization that this aim is at the heart of alchemy, of magic, and of religion provides the orientation not only for the individual, but for society as a whole, unifying man and nature, the individual and society, the highest and the lowest, in one aim: the realization of man as Angel, as Mind.

It is for this that all – not only magic and alchemy – exists.

THE HEEL
OF ACHILLES

It might seem superfluous to add any caveat regarding the dangers of sorcery, the dangers having been amply reiterated over the course of the centuries in the West, but there are several aspects of – or better, inversions of – magic as the natural irradiation of a tradition which ought to be emphasized since they have not been sufficiently noted, and since they are directly related to the peculiar circumstances of our modern era. For in fact the question is not only a matter of the dangers *to* magic – since it, like all traditional disciplines and arts is increasingly endangered, seemingly destined to become extinct in our brave new and 'sanitized' world – but also a matter of the dangers *of* 'magic': that is, of its inversion in 'psychism,' sorcery and the false mysticism of the emerging 'counter-tradition.'

Indeed, the peculiar nature of our modern era, which has been so penetratingly analysed in the works of René Guénon,[1] colours, or perhaps better taints, nearly every aspect of our perception of the traditional cosmology – since we are today living in an almost uncompromisingly dualistic society. Consequently, we must be more cautious when approaching spiritual discipline in general and theurgy in particular, for ours is indisputably a time in which, as is written in the New Testament, false prophets are many, and they may shew

120

wonders to deceive, if it were possible, even the elect. Hence mere unusual phenomena must never be accepted as being only a result of spiritual training, though they may be, and though we have in general so approached them. For, given the nature of our times, such phenomena might also arise about those whose aims are the very antithesis of spiritual in order to 'substantiate' their pseudotradition, which can be but the inversion of sacred traditions, leading away from the Sun of Divine reality rather than towards it. One must be ever vigilant against hubris.

Of course, this has to an extent been the case for some time – Abramelin, who lived in fifteenth-century Europe and Ko Hung, who lived in fourth-century China concur above all in one thing: the prevalence of charlatans and deceivers. But the situation today is somewhat graver in that nearly everything at the apparent terrestrial level is becoming ever more unstable: culture, the medium or mesocosm between man and the macrocosm, has by and large disintegrated under the pressure of the modern era, leaving individuals without the moorings to perform even in daily life without being impaired by confusion and anxiety, much less to function – and not be disastrously overwhelmed by malevolent or 'infernal' forces – in the realm of theurgy.

And as the modern era continues its inevitable course towards complete immersion in the blindness to all but matter and, ironically,[2] toward complete divorce from the natural world, the rare individual who can penetrate even to the point of perceiving the existence of the realms of the celestial will still be very much affected by the confusion, anxiety and ignorance of his age – all of which leaves one very much open to becoming prey to the malevolent forces or influences which do indeed exist in the cosmos just as they exist within the individual.

All of this leads to the inescapable conclusion that one must be more on guard now than ever before – and this is even more true of one following the primordial path, as he attracts both the positive and negative aspects of existence more strongly than the ordinary person. This need for caution in fact formed the crux of the greatest dilemma Dr John Dee and Sir Edward Kelley, in the sixteenth century, faced with the conjuration of spirits: were the voices and apparitions those of the 'evil' realm

121

masquerading as 'good,' or were they in truth Angelic and beneficent?[3] This is of course no mean question: it is one which in various ways we must all ask. By what force or tendency is that which we see and do guided?

On the other hand, we must keep in mind, too, that one on the primordial Way is by definition one who is closer to the celestial realms, and consequently must be more aware than most of that which is influencing his actions and the events around him. For true evil arises not from knowledge, but from ignorance. How many criminals, for instance, have said that they committed their acts because 'a voice' told them to do so? What, one must ask, is the real nature of such a 'voice?' Needless to say, one who is following the traditional Path is more aware of the source of such a 'voice' and consequently more equipped to deal with it; indeed, only within the sphere of traditional religion is there sanctuary.

But be this as it may, one must in this modern era strive to be most keenly aware of the true nature of that with which one is dealing. For as it is written in the Surangama Sutra, in the last epoch after the Buddha's Parinirvana, there will be heretics abounding both within one and without. These, it is said, will be composed of three grades: those who tempt one to power and pride; those who tempt one to erudition; and the common heretics who simply confuse. Some of these goblin-heretics will then, it is said, even 'hide themselves within the very personalities of the saints in order to carry out their deceiving tricks.' If this is true of holy men and saints, how much more must it be true of most – who live in the midst of the realm of Mara and delusion and know it not? And as the modern era – the last epoch of this world – draws to a close, the goblins of ego will necessarily gain ever greater sway.

Those forces in the modern era which led to the destruction of the traditional cultures – that is, to the emerging anti-tradition which is the central characteristic and motive force of this era – those forces of division and disintegration adversely affect not only the perception of individuals, but also change the very nature of certain areas and monuments which were once sacred, causing them, as it were, to radiate malevolent force or influence. In fact, many modern buildings are in themselves manifestations of this anti-traditional influence, standing almost wholly against the natural laws of beauty, proportion and symmetric harmony, a most conspicuous display of egotism and of near-total divorce from nature.

Guénon, in his *The Reign of Quantity and the Signs of the Times* (1953), spoke of precisely this kind of inversion of the sacred which is the culmination, so to speak, of the course of the modern era – since it is only logical that once the traditionally sacred has 'lost its power' the next step is for it to become, or rather, be supplanted by the inverted anti-tradition. It is not mere happenstance that another name for Satan or Iblis is 'the ape of God.' In Guénon's vision the traditional culture is seen as being enclosed in a kind of sacred sphere which protects it from malevolent forces and which allows that culture to remain in a harmonious orbit around the Sun of existence. But in the modern era, this sphere is being progressively rent asunder, allowing those forces whose primary aim is *away* from the Sun, *away* from the traditional, to gain sway and to wreak havoc.

One consequence of this tendency of our modern era is that once-sacred areas – like the many false prophets and teachers – act as the very antithesis of their original, traditional purpose, acting for the prevailing anti-tradition, and increasing blindness, confusion and egotism under the very guise of the sacred. It is not insignificant that precisely those areas of the world which were once the most influential spiritual centers – such as Persia, India, and the Near East – are now very much associated with the most extreme fanaticism and violence: almost the exact inversion of the relative peace and harmony of the traditional cultures.

A gross example of this transformation of the sacred, of even religious symbols into anti-traditional symbols, is of course the swastika, which was a very ancient and sacred symbol appropriated by the Nazis, and which thereby came to symbolize the greatest triumph of brutality and egotism the world has yet known. But there are numerous other, often subtler, instances of the same kind of symbolic misappropriation and inversion, some with a much longer history indeed.

There are also, increasingly, a number of more blatantly malevolent movements which, despite their avowed 'good intentions,' are very much associated with – both creations of and creators of – forces and influences which might well be termed demonic or evil, as signified by their acceptance of animal sacrifice in order to satisfy their 'personal gods.' These 'gods,' needless to say, bear a close affinity with the 'voices' which criminals are said to often hear, and which we mentioned earlier. These movements bear many characteristics of the traditional, including priests, periods of purification, and so on: but dedicated to what end? Personal power, suffering, egoism.

Considering the nature of our modern era as that which the Hindus termed *kali yuga*, and that which the Buddha called 'the last five hundred years,' considering the progressive fragmentation and even atomization of our world in this era, it is not at all surprising that such movements – and those malevolent forces which both spawn and are spawned by them – are increasing in number and in intensity, or perhaps ferocity is a better word. Evil feeds upon that which is released when blood is shed. That is one reason that Buddhists – like many medicine men and 'native religions' – observe abstinence from the eating of meat at least during periods of purification.

All of this, once again, points to an inescapable conclusion which everyone drawn to the traditional disciplines must take into account: ours is an era in which not only does the stability and order of the traditional culture not hold sway, but indeed it is a time when the very antithesis of the traditional – the thrust toward chaos, division, disintegration and the reign of quantity – affects nearly every aspect of existence.

On the one hand, this means that the magus must be extraordinarily cautious, in order that he not be affected by this most dangerous of Achilles' heels – the reductionism, blindness and egoism of the modern era. And yet, conversely, the spiritual desolation of the modern era does leave much of the natural realm crying out as it were for the regenerative healing power which the theurge can provide, drawing things once again into their natural orbits, their natural harmony. As Lame Deer, a modern Sioux medicine man, has said – we moderns ignore the symbolic aspects of our life. Our daily existence itself is necessarily the highest manifestation of the spiritual, if only we could see it so, and it is this kind of healing – the uniting of the spiritual and the mundane, the celestial and the quotidian – that is, ultimately, the highest task of the magus.

In the words of Rilke, 'we are the bees of the invisible,' our task being above all the transmutation of the familiar things of

124

this world into the transcendent, the Divine. And although our world is increasingly being flooded with sham objects, facsimiles of the natural realm — synthetic apples, synthetic vegetables, antiseptic houses and the sterility of lawns, to name but a few — yet even so that transformation of our world into the simultaneous stellar realm, that transformation of which magic is necessarily an aspect, is still open to us inasmuch as we are open to it.

It is true that in the modern era this is most difficult, perhaps more difficult than at any other time. But on the other hand it is also true that where the greatest obstacles lie, there too lies the greatest potential.

For the greatest danger to us shall arise, not because of 'magic,' but rather if true magic, true transmutation, should disappear.[4]

That is the true 'heel of Achilles.'

AFTERWORD

The ultimate gauge of a culture must be the extent to which magic and religion are merged and harmonized in the individual spiritual path it presents, magic or 'Divine affinity' being its effect; religion being its formal unity. Without a unified religion, magic becomes mere superstition, while without magic, religion degenerates into a sterile and barbaric dogmatism. Magic and religion, then, form a polarity; each invigorates the other. From the polarity between the solitary and the communal arises a higher union which can be glimpsed in Zen Buddhism, Tantrism, Sūfism, and Taoism – those who are at the apex of their tradition, and embody both the ritual form – the communal – and the individual experience – the solitary spirit – transcending the duality of form and content, religion and magic, so that ultimately nothing may be said of them at all.

If one conceives of the relation between magic and religion as a hierarchic triangle, then at its apex must be those highest forms of religion which transcend that duality, and the categorization of magic and religion itself, constantly transcending and reinvigorating as well as being the culmination of their own tradition. Below these, then, must be those traditions which, like Taoism, came to be divided between orthodox priests who were magicians, and unorthodox magicians. This polarity forced the orthodoxy to be continually assimilating the unorthodox magicians' technique in order that the orthodox would not be overwhelmed, overpowered by the unorthodox. At this level of the triangle, there is no real resolution, as there is at the apex; on the other hand, the essential unity, the reciprocal nature of magic and religion, has not been lost. Each 'side' – orthodox and unorthodox – learns from and revitalizes the other.

At the base of the triangle, however, are the two lowest forms of magic and religion, which at this point have degenerated from a polarity into an antithesis, so that rather than renewing one another, magic and religion became wholly at odds, with orthodoxy and its numbers and temporal power forever emerging the bloody victor. Both of the most base forms of magic and religion are contaminated by egotism, and by the consequent search for and reliance upon that which is external, be it demons, in magic, or an external savior, in religion. At the left base of the hierarchic triangle is the base struggle for egotistic ends, for greed and power attainment through magic – which is of course a contradiction in terms and a denial of the essence of magic – while on the right is sterile and rigid dogmatism – which of course becomes a denial of the essence of religion as the quest for the Divine. Only in the West – in the Judeo-Christian tradition – did the living polarity between magic and religion descend into a destructive antithesis which blunted the transmission of divine knowledge and the experience of Reality at the heart of both magic and religion. It is worthwhile to note that the two lowest forms of magic and religion at the base of the triangle, those characterized by the egotistic quest for dominance, are also marked by the demand that one *believe*. Believe, says the magician; believe, say the dogmatist.

But, as Plato said, belief is the inferior of knowledge and must forever be subsumed to it. True magic, like true religion, can only be founded upon the individual experience of it, for which religion provides the form and magic the content. And try as the dogmatists may to exterminate it, in magic is reflected the purpose and meaning of human existence – man as microcosm – and it cannot be exterminated without the consequent extirpation of all human meaning and purpose. One can, however, come to understand how the antipathy

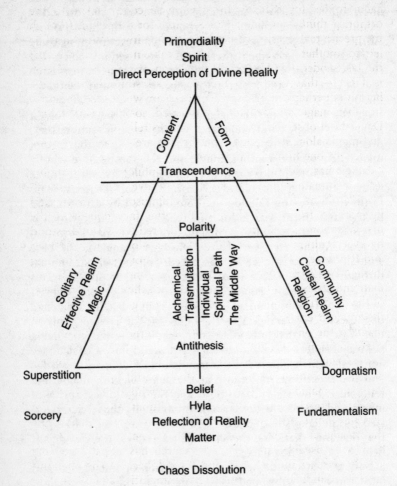

Primordiality
Spirit
Direct Perception of Divine Reality

Content   Form

Transcendence

Polarity

Solitary   Alchemical   Community
Effective Realm   Transmutation   Causal Realm
Magic   Individual   Religion
                  Spiritual Path
                  The Middle Way

Antithesis

Superstition   Dogmatism

Belief
Hyla
Reflection of Reality
Matter

Sorcery   Fundamentalism

Chaos Dissolution

XIII The relation of religion and magic

between the solitary magician and the bureaucratic orthodoxy came to be, for the solitary cannot be controlled – so the orthodox think – in his relentless search for the Divine, though the precise reasons this conflict came to be in the West must be left to another volume. It is, in any case, no coincidence that the last modern land to retain the union of magic and religion is Tibet – that vast and snowy land of solitude, where the hermit is perhaps more prevalent than anywhere else on earth. In Tibet, magic and religion are married, so that as Alexandra David-Neel observed, the monk practices religion communally, and magic alone in his quarters; the two are in harmony, being aspects of one human transmutation.

Magic has seldom, if ever, been given philosophical standing as a legitimate philosophical vision – save perhaps through Neoplatonism, and in the East, where philosophy is in any case inseparable from religion – despite the fact that it is the manifestation of a vision, a system adhered to and understood by every culture in the world. That fact alone lends it power and legitimacy. The reason that magic is not in good standing in the West is that it is based upon the fundamental unity of man and cosmos and so is in conflict with the inherent dualism of the modern outlook. But magic will be in existence long after the modern era has disappeared: it cannot be otherwise, for magic is the physical expression of the eternal, inner, spiritual transmutation.

Yet magic demands a living religion; without that living religion it cannot survive, and this, perhaps, explains the decline of magic in the West. For, today, who in the West takes angelic hierarchies seriously? Magic, ultimately, is justified in two ways: first, because it tantalizes one toward the Divine, like the promised magical sword which, when finally attained, cannot be used because the very search has transformed the greedy searcher into a saint; and second, because the phenomena surrounding the spiritual transmutation of man are necessarily magical inasmuch as magic is the natural result of ascent above the temporal into the Eternal, hence being an inevitable part of the spiritual path.

This study represents but the beginning of a unified understanding of magic and alchemy – it is an attempt to examine, in modern terms, that which underlies those phenomena known as magic and alchemy, subjects whose depths are immeasurable, since they veil and reveal the most immense journey imaginable: the journey of the soul toward the Divine. Inasmuch as this study orients one who is seeking is it, and may it be, of value.

But the final word on the subject may perhaps be that of Jacob Böehme, who in his *Six Theosophic Points* wrote as follows:

Magic is the mother of eternity, of the being of all beings, for it creates itself and is understood in desire.

Magic is spirit and being is its body; and yet the two are but one, as body and soul is but one person.

Magic is the greatest secrecy, for it is above Nature and makes Nature after the form of its will. It is the mystery of the Ternary – that is, it is in desire the will striving toward the heart of God.

In Magic are all forms of Being of all beings. It is a mother in all three worlds, and makes each thing after the model of that thing's will. It is not the understanding, but it is a creatrix according to the understanding, and lends itself to good or to evil.

It is Magic that makes divine flesh, and the understanding is born of wisdom, for it is a discerner of colours, powers, and virtues.

The senses are such a subtle spirit that they enter into all beings and take all beings up into themselves. But the understanding tries all in its own fire: it rejects the evil and retains the good. Then Magic, its mother, takes this and brings it into being.

Magic is the mother from which nature comes, and the understanding of it is the Mother coming from nature. Magic leads into a fierce fire, and the understanding leads its own mother, Magic, out of the fierce fire into its own fire.

Magic is without understanding and yet comprehends all; for it is the comprehension of all things.

APPENDICES

Tabula Iovis in abaco

4	14	15	1
9	7	6	12
5	11	10	8
16	2	3	13

Iovis

Intelligentiae
Iovis

Daemonij
Iovis

Appendix I The planetary tables and sigils

132

Tabula Martis in abaco

11	24	7	20	3
4	12	25	8	16
17	5	13	21	9
10	18	1	14	22
23	6	19	2	15

Martis

Intelligentiae Martis

Daemonij Martis

Tabula Solis in abaco

6	32	3	34	35	1
7	11	27	28	8	30
19	14	16	15	23	24
18	20	22	21	17	13
25	29	10	9	26	12
36	5	33	4	2	31

Solis

Intelligentiae Solis

Daemonij Solis

22	47	16	41	10	35	4
5	23	48	17	42	11	29
30	6	24	49	18	36	12
13	31	7	25	43	19	37
38	14	32	1	26	44	20
21	39	8	33	2	27	45
46	15	40	9	34	3	28

Veneris

Daemonij Veneris

Intelligentiarŭ
Veneris

Intelligentiarŭ
Veneris

Tabula Mercurij in abaco

8	58	59	5	4	62	63	1
49	15	14	52	53	11	10	56
41	23	22	44	45	19	18	48
32	34	35	29	28	38	39	25
40	26	27	37	36	30	31	33
17	47	46	20	21	43	42	24
9	55	54	12	13	51	50	16
64	2	3	61	60	6	7	57

Mercurij

Daemoniŭ Mercurij

Intelligentiae
Mercurij

Tabula Lunae in abaco

37	78	29	70	21	62	13	45	5
6	38	79	30	71	22	63	14	46
47	7	39	80	31	72	23	55	15
16	48	8	40	81	32	64	24	56
57	17	49	9	41	73	33	65	25
26	58	18	50	1	42	74	34	66
67	27	59	10	51	2	43	75	35
36	68	19	60	11	52	3	44	76
77	28	69	20	61	12	53	4	45

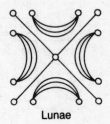

Lunae

Daemonij Lunae

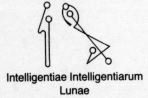

Intelligentiae Intelligentiarum
Lunae

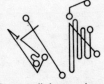

Daemonij daemoniorum
Lunae

APPENDICES

Appendix II   The natural calendar of John Trithemius (Johannis Tritemei), the mentor of Agrippa. The calendar is laden with meanings, being a correspondence chart, a calendar, and a repository of numerous recondite symbols – Hermetic, Qabalistic, Neoplatonic, and magical. Dated 1503, it is in the National Bibliotek, Vienna, Codex 11313.

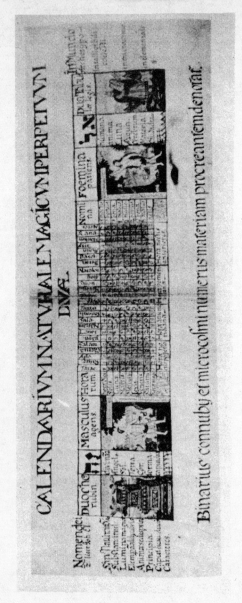

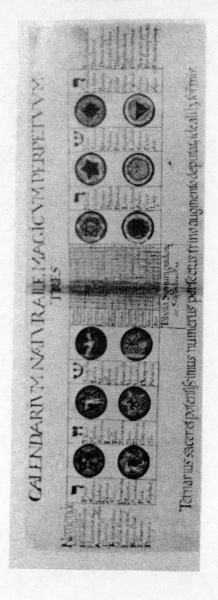

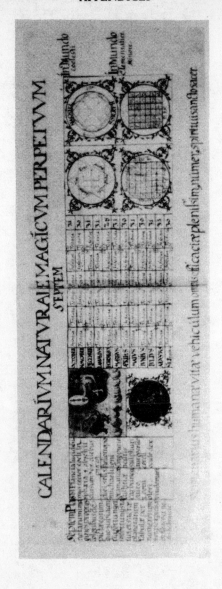

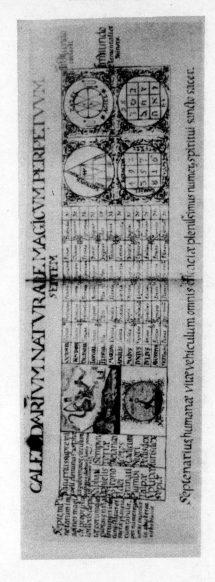

Appendix III The Hermetic Initiation, in *Tomi Secundi Tractatus
Primi, Sectio Secunda, De technica Microcosmi historia*, in *Portiones
Vii divisa*, Oppenheim, 1620, by Robert Fludd.

The direct transmission or revelation of *gnosis* by master to disciple
is the unequivocal *centrum* of which magic and alchemy are but
temporal aspects. It is with this – the essentiality of the experiential
revelation of Mind – that we both begin and end this study.

NOTES

PREFACE

1 It is instructive in this regard to examine the interrelationship of the magus and the Catholic church during the later medieval period, a time – prelude to the wholescale confusion, blindness and chaos of the present era – which amply illustrates this.

2 Both of these – manipulative science and the counter-tradition – are characterized by one tendency above all: the attempt by the ego or psyche to assume functions which are Transcendent or Divine, an attempt best characterized by the word 'satanic' – that is, the 'human' usurping the place of the Divine, attempting to become Creator. The false mysticism of the counter-tradition leads to chaos and dissolution of the self; science leads to solipsism – but ultimately these amount as it were to the same thing. The conjunction of these two can be glimpsed in present attempts to unite the seemingly endless 'particularizations' of physics with the self-dissolution of false mysticism.

3 It is with this aim in mind that we chose the title of this work, the word 'philosophy' being intended, not in its present decadent sense of mere abstract reasoning, but in its original meanings as 'attraction toward wisdom' and, more

151

widely interpreted, the 'application' or 'effects on life' of wisdom – both of which admirably describe the nature of magic within a primordial culture.

Likewise, the word 'magic' refers to the divine affinity and sympathetic harmony which is natural to the primordial tradition – in the West transmitted as 'Hermeticism' – and in no wise must this be confused with its inverted image, seen in 'sorcery,' 'psychism' and the modern purveyors of false tradition and false mysticism, the myriad pseudo-gurus and would-be 'teachers' and 'heads of orders.'

This emerging 'counter-tradition' flourishes in proportion as people begin to recognize the barrenness of merely 'materialistic' existence, drawing upon the much-venerated delusions of 'evolution' and 'progress' to promise 'new powers' to a 'new man' in a 'new age,' but leading people in reality downward toward the subconscious and subhuman, toward con-fusion and dissolution in the ocean of Chaos – the very inverse of the re-union with the Divine at the center of the primordial tradition.

INTRODUCTION

1 The Christian expression 'loss of the soul' (Greek:psyche) corresponds to a very real condition – that is, the psyche is lost in illusion, and eventually 'dissolves.'

2 In the same vein, pursuit of the prolongation or 'empowering' of the individual through a pseudo-tradition leads to his eventual dissolution, whereas a genuine tradition leads to his 'flowering,' to revelation of his Divine nature *in* individuality.

3 See H. Corbin, *Avicenna and the Visionary Recital* (New York, 1960) as well as S.H. Nasr's *An Introduction to Islamic Cosmological Doctrines* (Cambridge, 1964).

4 See Frances Yates, *Giordano Bruno and the Hermetic Tradition* (London, 1964), as well as *The Ash Wednesday Supper* by A. Versluis.

5 See 'Selections from *Pollen and Fragments*,' Novalis, A. Versluis, trs., in *Temenos*, Kathleen Raine (ed.) (London, 1986).

6 See Plotinus, 'Against the Gnostics', in *The Enneads*, S.

MacKenna, trs. (London, 1962).

7 Cf. Lama Govinda, *Foundations of Tibetan Mysticism* (London, 1960).

8 From *The Secret of the Golden Flower*, R. Wilhelm and C.G. Jung (New York, 1931). For a discussion of the Jungian inversion of traditional metaphysics see Titus Burckhardt's *Alchemy: Science of the Cosmos, Science of the Soul* (London, 1967).

9 Chuang Tsu, *Inner Writings*, B. Watson, trs. (New York, 1964).

10 Muhammad Tunikābunī, *Qisas al-'ulamā*, from S.H. Nasr's *An Introduction to Islamic Cosmological Doctrines* (Cambridge, 1964), p. 194.

11 *Discourse on the Eighth and Ninth*, Codex VI, 58, *Nag Hammadi Library* (New York, 1977), p. 295.

PART I THE PHILOSOPHY OF MAGIC

1 See Frances Yates, *The Art of Memory* (London, 1966), and *Giordano Bruno and the Hermetic Tradition* (London, 1964) in which the introduction of the *Poimandres* into the West is recognized as the inception of the Renaissance, and its discrediting as the decline of the Renaissance.

2 See W.Y. Evans Wentz, *Tibetan Yoga and Secret Doctrines* (Oxford, 1958), pp. 224-8 for a Tibetan explication of the Clear Light.

3 In Sūfism, the moon is seen as the focus of the planets; below it, on earth, is the realm of generation. See S.H. Nasr, *An Introduction to Islamic Cosmological Doctrines*, pp. 160-2. The moon's number is 28, the numbers of the planets $(1+2+3+4+5+6+7)$ added.

4 See *Zen Master Dogen* by Yuho Yukoi (New York, 1976).

5 See the works of Gershom Scholem – in particular his history of Jewish mysticism and his work on Messianic Judaism and Qabalism.

6 See Michael Saso, *The Teachings of Taoist Master Chuang* (Yale, 1978) for a study of contemporary Taoism, and its history.

7 Thich Nhat Hanh, *Zen Keys* (New York, 1978).

8 See the Robert Fludd diagrams of the head and hand

symbolism. In Ficino and Agrippa the microcosmic associations are very localized, as they are in Taoist magic.

9 That ritual hand movements are a Western as well as Eastern magical practice can be seen in the rare manuscripts reproduced in the following chapter.

10 *Girardius Parvi Lucii libellus de mirabilibus naturae arcanis*, Anna Domini 1730, ms. 3009, Bibliothèque de l'Arsenal, Paris.

11 See Lama Govinda's *Foundations of Tibetan Mysticism* (London, 1960) for an examination of the harmonic relation of words and sounds to the celestial realm.

12 See David Fideler, *The Song of Apollo* (Grand Rapids, 1984) and W. Stirling, *The Canon* (London, 1897).

13 See Henry Corbin, *Avicenna and the Visionary Recital* (New York, 1960) and his *Spiritual Body, Celestial Earth* (Princeton, 1977). See also the candle imagery in the diagrams included in John Dee's *The Hieroglyphic Monad* (New York, 1975).

14 Alexandra David-Neel, *Magic and Mystery in Tibet* (New York, 1960).

15 In this we can glimpse the way in which the arising counter-tradition 'apes' the primordial tradition: in the false mysticism of the pseudo-gurus and others the ego is 'dissolved' and 'time and space annihilated' as they lead their followers down into chaos and dissolution; in the primordial tradition ego is transcended, gone beyond.

16 Jacob Böehme, *The Aurora* (London, 1964).

17 Michael Saso, *op. cit.*

18 Alexandra David-Neel, *The Secret Oral Teachings In Tibetan Buddhist Sects* (San Francisco, 1967).

19 See Michael Saso, *op. cit.*

20 The term 'Intellect' is used in the sense Giordano Bruno used it: as the *mens*, or both rational and suprarational faculty, both human and angelic.

21 See G.R.S. Mead, *Orpheus* (London, 1912) for a discussion of the Orphic Egg.

22 *Ibid*. The fish is the soul, which escapes from its blind entrapment in the net of matter.

23 The 'Gate of Life', in Taoism, is that celestial opening which must be sealed before magic can take place. See Saso, *op. cit.*

24 For more on the nature of this universal language see Keith Critchlow, *The Soul as Sphere and Androgyne* (Ipswich, 1980) and *Islamic Patterns: An Analytical and Cosmological Approach* (New York, 1976). See also the works of David Fideler and of Anne Macauley (forthcoming).

25 Cf. *de Occulta Philosophia*, H.C. Agrippa (Graz, 1967) in particular.

26 From the *Nei P'ien* of Ko Hung, in *Religion, Medicine and Alchemy* in the *China of 320 A.D.*, James Ware, tr. (New York, 1981), p. 54.

27 The Gnostic demiurge was a mythic depiction of ego and its blindness, not merely a fanciful, external and malignant deity, as many seem to think. But one must keep in mind that Gnosticism arose in a confused era, and was not, strictly speaking, traditional in nature.

28 See S.H. Nasr, *op. cit.*, for a discussion of traditional astrology in contradistinction to the modern form.

29 From Giordano Bruno's *Sigillus Sigillorum*. A memory wheel is reprinted in Frances Yate's *The Art of Memory* (London, 1966).

30 The great Tibetan yogi Milarepa was in fact inspired to become a student of the renowned Marpa, and enter the religious life, after having committed murder by means of black magic, and then having realized the immense evil he had thereby brought upon himself through that very 'black magic.' Cf. *Tibet's Great Yogi Milarepa*, W.Y. Evans-Wentz (ed.) (Oxford, 1928).

31 See Michael Saso, *op. cit.*, and Henry Corbin, *Spiritual Body and Celestial Earth* (Princeton, 1964).

32 See *Burnham's Celestial Handbook*, Vol. III (New York, 1978).

33 Philip Kapleau, *The Three Pillars of Zen* (New York, 1966).

34 Michael Saso, *op. cit.*

35 W.Y. Evans-Wentz (ed.), *The Tibetan Book of the Dead* (London, 1927).

36 For an elaboration of this aspect of traditional teaching – the relation of ancient architecture and geometry in particular – see Keith Critchlow, *Islamic Patterns: An Analytical and Cosmological Approach* (New York, 1976)

and David Fideler, *The Song of Apollo* (Grand Rapids, 1984).

37 For a discussion of the esoteric meaning of the cross, see René Guénon's *The Symbolism of the Cross* (London, 1946).

38 It must be kept in mind, however, that the term 'eternity' is merely provisional, referring primarily to the celestial and more enduring level of the phenomenal world, since ultimately one can say neither that there is 'eternity' nor that there is not.

39 See the diagram X on p. 67.

40 The other squares and sigils are reproduced in Appendix I.

41 A word no doubt derived from the Arabic, as was much of the Qabalistic tradition.

42 For an elaboration upon the method of sigil formation, see Francis King's introduction to *The Grimoire of Armadel* (London, 1980), as well as the work of David Fideler (unpublished) on the subject.

43 See the end of the *Republic*, when Plato discusses banishing the poets from his perfect kingdom. His point, in part — although the section is somewhat ironic — is that the poet must not reflect the material, but invoke the celestial realm.

44 See Lama Govinda, *Foundations of Tibetan Mysticism* (London, 1960) and Pierre Rambach, *The Secret Message of Tantric Buddhism* (Geneva, 1979).

45 J. Böehme, *op. cit.*, pp. 722-3.

46 Cf. René Guénon's *The Reign of Quantity and the Signs of the Times* (London, 1953). In the primordial culture these all act toward the deliverance of beings. But in the modern inversion of tradition and magic, these two 'psychic rings' are used infernally, drawing upon the residues left by past generations and cultures in order to 'create' their infernal mirror-image or 'counter-tradition' which instead of drawing upward toward Unity leads downward into dissent, dissolution, fear and Chaos.

47 See the *Nei P'ien* of Ko Hung, translated by James Ware (Cambridge, 1966) under the title *Alchemy, Medicine and Religion in the China of 320 A.D.*, for a Taoist discussion of earth spirits.

48 See Part II, 'Acclimation and tranquillity.'

49 See the writings of E. Wallis Budge and Henry Corbin.

50 This 'double' must never be conceived of as an extension or a reflection of the corporeal self, but rather, the latter must be seen as a 'reflection' of 'it.'

51 Particularly in New York, connected with 'voodoo' or 'neoshamanism.'

52 Abraham ben Samuel Abulafia, *The Path of the Names*, David Meltzer (ed.) (Tree, 1976).

53 *Tibet's Great Yogi Milarepa*, W.Y. Evans-Wentz (ed.) (London, 1928).

54 NHL (New York, 1977).

55 Martin Lings, *A Modern Sufi Saint: Shaikh Al'Alawi* (Berkeley, 1972).

56 The term 'theosophical' is used in its original, pure sense: as the elder of philosophy.

57 J. Böehme, *Six Theosophic Points* (Ann Arbor, 1960), p. 201.

58 As Nicolai Berdaeyev, in the introduction to the work quoted above, misguidedly attempted to do.

59 *Ibid*.

60 *Timaeus* (10:42).

61 Although in pure 'primordiality' – as for a Zen Buddhist master – such dualism no longer obtains, for one is then in the realm of 'skillful means.'

62 This is strongly suggested by both Macrobius and Proclus. See especially Macrobius's references to Orphism in his *Commentary on the Dream of Scipio* (New York, 1972).

63 J. Böehme, *The Aurora*, op. cit., p. 306.

64 See, for example the instructions in *The Sword of Moses* (London, 1896) or *The Clavicle of Solomon*, S.L. MacGregor Mathers, trs. (London, 1888) and *The Book of the Sacred Magic of Abramelin the Mage*, S.L. MacGregor Mathers, trs. (London, 1900).

65 See the forthcoming works of Anne Macauley on the Pythagorean harmonies and the origins of Apollo's lyre.

66 *Opera*, Marsilio Ficino, III, ii, 533.

67 Michael Saso, *op. cit*.

PART II THE IRRADIATION OF MAGIC

1 Each culture constitutes a 'world' in itself, simultaneously,

being inasmuch as it is pure a reflection of tradition primordial, the 'Golden Age.'

2 This 'boundlessness,' above the realm of psyche, is intimately related to the Hermetic teaching of the 'dancing harmony of the spheres' in the stellar or celestial realm, and in this we can glimpse the original, higher meaning of the celebratory dance of the Sabbat: it belongs to the realm of contemplative revelation, not temporal revelry.

3 Cf. René Guénon, *The Reign of Quantity and the Signs of the Times* (London, 1953).

4 In this regard Plotinus used the term 'autotelos.'

5 Cf. Plato's *Timaeus*, XI, on the sensory confusion of the soul. Here Mars, originally signifying courage, may 'become' anger and dissension.

6 That is, in the soul by virtue of its 'descent' into the sublunar material realm, the inherent duality of which causes planetary influences to be in disarray, therein, by reflective distortion as it were. The planets *themselves*, being divine, remain harmonious.

7 As A.K. Coomaraswamy pointed out in *The Transformation of Nature in Art* (London, 1934), the angels which dance upon the head of a pin in traditional terms can all be said to be concentrated upon a single point – the *axis mundi* – being as they are 'above' the phenomenal realm. But that the expression 'how many angels . . ?' has become common parlance is succinct indication of our ignorance of that realm.

8 The widespread use of hallucinogenic drugs and 'isolation tanks' suggests just how far in this direction things have already gone; related examples could be adduced almost indefinitely.

9 These are but prefigurations as it were of the emerging 'counter-tradition' of false mysticism which is the inverse of the primordial culture in every way, leading downward into the abyss of chaos and dissolution of the ego and soul, rather than upward toward unity and the Light.

10 See E. Wallis Budge, *Amulets and Talismans* (Cambridge, 1930), pp. 423, 488.

11 The tenor of this sentence suggests that it was added as a kind of talisman to ward off the malevolent influences of the Inquisition.

12 *Corpus Hermeticum*, A.J. Festugière (ed.) (Paris, 1945-54), II, 347 (Asc. xiii, 37).

13 *Macrobius' Commentary on the Dream of Scipio*, W.H. Stahl (ed.) (New York, 1952), p. 166.

14 W. Shumacher, *The Occult Sciences in the Renaissance* (London, 1972), p. 98.

15 As an illustration, Michael Saso tells of Master Chuang directing a drunken man compassionately from a party, ignoring the anger of his family and friends. See *The Teachings of Taoist Master Chuang, op. cit.*

16 *Op. cit.* pp. 179-94.

17 A protection which unfortunately is not granted to more recent attempts at 'seances,' 'spiritualism' or 'shamanism,' which involve laying oneself open to whatever seizes the opportunity.

18 This universal reciprocity or mirroring, which is necessary from a more 'elevated' point of view in order to complete a cycle, is suggested in the illustration by T. Campanella in the appendices which depicts 'impotentia' as the antithetical image of 'potential,' the former being necessary to 'complete' the latter.

19 The shift from one *Manvantara* to another implies a 'barrier' of physical, but not causal, discontinuity.

20 John Aubrey, *Three Prose Works* (Carbondale, 1972).

21 Indeed a supreme irony.

22 Marlowe's entire play consisted in a deliberate vulgarization of magic in order to discredit it, as well as Dr John Dee, the preeminent magus of the day, and so contributed to the widespread rejection of traditional cosmology which characterizes the present era.

23 'Illusory' here means not non-existent, but rather something neither real nor unreal, possessing only a provisional or conditional reality.

24 See *The Books* (New York, 1941), and the journal, *Fortean Times*, for numerous instances of similar phenomena.

25 W.Y. Evans-Wentz (ed.), *Tibetan Yoga and Secret Doctrines* (Oxford, 1933), p. 185.

26 In this regard one is reminded also of the Tibetan Buddhist *herukas* and *dakinis*, whose flaming limbs are similarly a 'mode' of purification and transmutation.

27 Cf. *The Tree That Never Dies*, P. Dobson (ed.), pp. 84ff.

28 Cf. Frank Waters, *Book of the Hopi* (New York, 1963), pp. 245-7.

29 Cf. E. Hall, *The Eskimo Storyteller: Folktales from Noatak Alaska* (Knoxville, 1975), for an indication of the *anatquq's* function in a world still 'magical.'

30 Even though by this point in history the present 'final' cycle had already begun, there was nonetheless a closer proximity to the primordial as attested to by the continuation, albeit attenuated, of the Mystery and Orphic traditions.

31 It is unfortunate that neither the 'myth of Er' nor the 'dream of Scipio' are often studied in modern examinations of Plato or Cicero, for they are at the heart of the two works and not, as several modern commentators have mistakenly indicated, spurious, superfluous additions. Indeed, the presence of the 'myth of Er' and the 'dream of Scipio' in these works should suggest that the entire works be read not only on a literal, but on an analogical or symbolic level as well, so that the works are also seen as encoded instructions, so to speak, for liberation from the tyranny of ego.

32 Indeed, strictly speaking it is both the source of and the only evil.

33 In this regard one is reminded of the longevity of Methuselah – and the Taoist sages – as of the millenium mentioned in the *Revelation* of John, all of which refer to a state of virtual immortality, or transcendence 'lasting' one cycle.

34 See *The Diamond Sutra*, A.F. Price and Wang Mou-Lam, (Berkeley, 1969) and its denial also of any 'soul' or illusory 'ego-entity.'

35 It is revealing that both fundamentalist dogmatic religion and the 'neoshaman' conceive of the soul in literalist temporal terms – and that the two have correspondingly ill-effects upon themselves and upon others. Indeed, both are manifestations of the same tendency.

PART III ALCHEMY

1 Titus Burckhardt, *Alchemy, Science of the Cosmos, Science of the Soul* (New York, 1971).

2 Lama Govinda, *Foundations of Tibetan Mysticism* (London, 1960).

3 See *Alchemy: Pre-Egyptian Legacy, Post-Millenial Promise*, R. Grossinger (ed.) (Richmond, 1979).

4 Elias Ashmole, *Theatrum Chemicum Brittanicum*, (London, 1652).

5 *A Testament of Alchemy*, ed. Lee Stavenhagen (Hanover, 1974).

6 Edward Kelly, *The Theatre of Terrestrial Astronomy* (London, 1676).

7 *Ibid.*

8 H. Corbin, *Spiritual Body, Celestial Earth* (Princeton, 1964).

9 From the 'Apocryphal Acts of Thomas,' in Hans Jonas, *The Gnostic Religion* (Boston, 1963).

10 Kelly was, like Bruno, a man behind much of the Renaissance, as even the preface to Spenser's *Shepherd's Calendar* shows – for it was written by one E.K., a close friend of Spenser's, and in the notes refers to Christ as Pan, all of which strongly suggests E.K. was Kelly, very much a force behind the scene.

11 Basilius Valentinus in 'The Triumphal Chariot of Antinomy' in R. Grossinger (ed.), *op. cit.*

12 See, for instance, the biography of Milarepa, Evans-Wentz (ed.) (Oxford, 1928). However, one must keep in mind that whereas Kelly stood at the end of a traditional era, and was not part of any initiatic transmission, the Tibetan *lama* stands within the continuity, the stream of tradition, and so can, under certain circumstances, make apparently outrageous suggestions in order to break one free from conceptual attachments – quite the opposite of one who seeks only to disrupt the established order for the sake of rebellion. The one seeks to liberate from attachment, the other to increase it – and it is difficult, given the intervening centuries, to tell where Kelly stands between the two.

THE HEEL OF ACHILLES

1 Cf. in particular Guénon's *The Reign of Quantity and the Signs of the Times* (London, 1953).

2 Ironically enough, this divorce from the natural world, this descent into blindness is celebrated by Teilhard de Chardin, in whose works even nuclear obliteration is seen as a sign of human 'evolution' and 'progress,' perhaps the ultimate in evolutionist absurdity. For an examination of the difference between the traditional teaching of emanation and modern evolutionism, see S.H. Nasr's *Knowledge and the Sacred* (New York, 1981).

3 John Dee, *A True and Faithful Relation of What Occurred Between Dr John Dee and Some Spirits*, I Casaubon (ed.) (London, 1659).

4 It is worthwhile to note while discussing our present era that we are indeed entering a new Platonic 'Great Year' cycle, beginning with the 'age of Aquarius,' but far from signifying a 'New Age' as some naively hope, Aquarius in reality is the Great Month most adverse to human life, denoting the flood of ignorance – ruled by Saturn – overwhelming all. Cf. in this regard Macrobius's observation to this effect in this *Commentary on the Dream of Scipio*, (New York, 1972), XII, as well as Thomas Taylor's translation of Porphyry's *De Antro Nympharum* in *Thomas Taylor The Platonist*, Kathleen Raine (ed.) (London, 1969), pp. 310-11, 321. We might here add that the Path – and its divine affinities, or magic – can never truly disappear of course, but nonetheless from a temporal point of view it can become obscured indeed.

SELECT
BIBLIOGRAPHY

Rather than simply listing the works with a bearing upon this
study, it seems appropriate to offer a brief commentary as
well, due to the nature of the subject. Not surprisingly, the
number of serious works on magic and alchemy is relatively
small, and even fewer undertake to present the subject
without the veneer of rationalistic cynicism which so
handicaps the enquiry into suprarational subjects. For an
overview of magic and alchemy, two useful works are
Witchcraft, Magic and Alchemy (New York, 1931) by Grillot
de Givry and *The Occult Sciences in the Renaissance*
(Berekeley, 1972) by Wayne Schumacher, though both are
severely limited in depth. Also useful are Kurt Seligmann's
The Mirror of Magic (New York, 1948), D.P. Walker's
Spiritual and Demonic Magic from Ficino to Campanella
(London, 1958), Lynn Thorndike's *A History of Magic and
Experimental Science* (New York, 1958) in eight volumes,
and of particular note are Frances Yates's books, beginning
with *Giordano Bruno and the Hermetic Tradition* (London,
1964). Yates is of particular importance in that she
approaches her subject with the intent of understanding it,
rather than juggling names. But the two most important
works for the understanding of these subjects, considering
the peculiar nature of our present era, are *The Crisis of the*

Modern World (London, 1942) and *The Reign of Quantity and the Signs of the Times* (London, 1953) by René Guénon. Texts pertaining to magic of particular interest include the *Anthroposophia theomagica*, and *Anima magica abscondita* (London, 1650), both by Thomas Vaughan; *A True and Faithful Relation of What Happened for Many Years between Dr John Dee and Some Spirits*, M. Casaubon (ed.) (London, 1659) which was intended to discredit Dee and Kelly; *Oedipus aegyptiacus*, by Athanasius Kircher (Rome, 1652), which, like Bruno before him, traces all wisdom, Oriental and Occidental, to Egypt. Of paramount importance, of course, are *De vita triplici*, by Marsilio Ficino, and *de Occulta Philosophia*, by Henry Cornelius Agrippa. The latter has been reprinted; Ficino is available only as Marsilius Ficinus Florentinus, *Opera* (Basiliae, 1576). Also of value are the texts known as *The Clavicle of Solomon*, and *The Book of the Sacred Magic of Abramelin the Mage*, M. Mathers, trs. (New York, 1900), among others. The latter is of particular importance in its depiction of Abraham's travels through medieval Europe and the Near East in search of a magus, as well as in its emphasis upon purity in magic.

As regards alchemy, the introductory text of preeminent importance must be Titus Burckhardt's *Alchemy: Science of the Cosmos, Science of the Soul* (London, 1967). Burckhardt presents the traditional view of alchemy as spiritual transmutation with great eloquence. In this vein, Lama Anagarika Govinda's *Foundations of Tibetan Mysticism* (London, 1960) is also irreplaceable as a study of Tibetan inner alchemy. Also of value is *Alchemy: pre-Egyptian Legacy, Millenial Promise* (Richmond, 1979), R. Grossinger, (ed.) in its selection of traditional alchemical texts, including Zosimos's and Paracelsus's writings. Unfortunately, the commentary is largely literalist and of limited value. A.E. Waite's *The Secret Tradition in Alchemy* (London, 1926), M.A. Atwood's *Hermetic Philosophy and Alchemy: A Suggestive Inquiry* (1850; New York, 1960) and *A Testament of Alchemy*, L. Stavenhagen (ed.) (Hanover 1974) are also of interest.

The literature on Neoplatonism, Hermeticism, and Gnosticism is fairly extensive; what follows is a listing of those works

which proved useful in the preparation of this work. Most
accessible is the *Nag Hammadi Library*, (New York, 1977),
a compilation of Gnostic texts discovered in 1945. The
writings of G.R.S. Mead are of great value as well – in
particular his *Thrice Greatest Hermes; Plotinus; Appolonius
of Tyana*; and *Fragments of a Faith Forgotten*, all published
in the early twentieth century, and most reprinted at least
once. Indeed, Mead is perhaps the student's best introduction
to this area. Unfortunately, much of the Neoplatonic
literature is unavailable; those which are include many of the
Thomas Taylor translations, including Iamblichus's *Life of
Pythagoras* and Proclus's *Two Treatises*. Also of value are
Macrobius's *Commentary on the Dream of Scipio*, W. Harris
Stahl, trs. (New York, 1972) and Proclus's *Elements of
Theology*, E.R. Dodds, trs. (Oxford, 1933). Of interest are
the works of Hans Jonas and Jacques LaCarrière on
Gnosticism. The best edition of the *Corpus Hermeticum*,
besides those of Mead and of Scott, is that of A.J. Festugière
(Paris, 1945). See also the works of Jacob Böehme – *The
Aurora* (London, 1960) and *Six Theosophic Points* (Ann
Arbor, 1958) in particular. For an introduction to the
transmission of the Hermetic and Neoplatonic tradition in
Islam, see S.H. Nasr's *An Introduction to Islamic
Cosmological Doctrines* (Harvard, 1964), as well as his
Knowledge and the Sacred (New York, 1981). See also the
works of Henry Corbin *in toto*. L. Massignon's *The Passion
of al-Hallaj: Mystic and Martyr of Islam* (Princeton, 1982)
(four vols) is of wider scope than its title would indicate. For
studies of Qabalism see the works of Gershom Scholem, as
well as the periodic publications of Tree Books, D. Meltzer
(ed.). Finally, a valuable source for rare Hermetic works is
Magnum Opus, 12 Antigua St, Edinburgh 1, Scotland, Adam
Mclean (ed.).

Literature on the Eastern traditions is truly immense; those
works which have proven to be of most help include *The
Dhammapada*, Narada There, trs. (London, 1954), *The
Lankavatara Sutra*, D.T. Suzuki, trs. (London, 1932), and *A
Buddhist Bible*, Dwight Goddard (Thetford, 1938), as well as
the writings of René Guénon, H.V. Guenther and W.Y.
Evans-Wentz. See, in particular, *The Tibetan Book of the
Dead, Tibet's Great Yogi Milarepa*, and *Tibetan Yoga and*

SELECT BIBLIOGRAPHY

Secret Doctrines, all edited by Evans-Wentz and published by Oxford, London.

Of great importance are the works of Lama Anagarika Govinda – especially his *Foundations of Tibetan Mysticism* (London, 1969), and *The Psychological Attitude of Early Buddhist Philosophy* (London, 1960). The works of Alexandra David-Neel, and *Magic and Mystery in Tibet* (London, 1958) above all, provide an introduction to Tibetan life, in which magic and religion are fused. The works of John Blofeld provide a similar and valuable introduction to Chinese Taoism. *The Teachings of Taoist Master Chuang* (New Haven, 1976) is also of great value, being an introduction to the actual practice of Taoist magic. As to Taoist texts, the best translation of the *Tao Te Ching* is that by Gia Fu Feng (New York, 1972); that by James Legge (*The Texts of Taoism*, Vols I and II (New York, 1891) is dated, but contains translations unavailable elsewhere. Notable among works on Zen Buddhism are the Ch'an series of Lu Kuan Yu and the works of Nyogen Senzaki, as well as K. Sekida's *Zen Training* (New York, 1975), Philip Kapleau's *The Three Pillars of Zen* (New York, 1965) *Golden Wind* (Tokyo, 1979) by Eido Shimano Roshi, and the series edited by Ruth Fuller Sasaki, including *The Record of Lin Chi* (Kyoto, 1975).

See also the *Nei P'ien* of Ko Hung, under the title *Religion, Medicine and Alchemy in the China of 320 A.D.*, J. Ware, trs. (New York, 1981).

Miscellaneous works of interest include the *Three Prose Works* of John Aubrey (Carbondale, 1972), and the works of E. Wallis Budge – in particular his *Egyptian Magic* (London, 1894) and *Amulets and Talismans* (Oxford, 1930).

INDEX

167